"I told him that I wanted to sail not to Canada but to St. Pierre off the coast, where we would be free and surrounded by both French women and the ocean. He told me that only an ijiot Irish fool would want to trade one cold island for another. He thought Australia might be the place to go. I said that was too far and honestly that I doubted the wisdom of running away only to end up on the bottom of the earth." – *This Dark*

"I say it again, "this is pretty much the end of the earth," and she just smiles. "Well, certainly," I admit, "there are the Faroes out lost in the fog somewhere beyond and even past that Iceland sure, but that's really only for Vikings and drunk Germans who like to get naked in the hot pools," and she just laughs." But really it is just wild water until it turns to ice and ice until you're going south again and the ice turns into Siberia." – *for Owen who did not think Donegal had proper beaches*

"You can only learn a place by walking. That is why the places you know from childhood are closest to you. And you can only know a city intimately by walking through its night. Then you see the secrets as the lighted rooms reveal themselves and the darkened shops speak without the affected accents they strive for while open. You see the cars of the residents and their trash, and without the purposeful sounds of planned life you can hear every argument, every cough, and even the cries." – *This Dublin Night*

Ira David Socol

A Certain Place of Dreams

very short stories

RIVER
FOYLE
PRESS

for Jill, who helps me find safe places

Ira David Socol

A Certain Place of Dreams

very short stories

Copyright 2007 by Ira Socol

A Certain Place of Dreams

First U.S. Printing by The River Foyle Press September 2007

ISBN-13: 978-0-6151-6369-7

ISBN-10: 0-6151-6369-7

www.riverfoylepress.com

riverfoylepress@gmail.com

Some stories have been previously published in slightly different forms, 2004-2007 on-line.

RIVER
FOYLE
PRESS

Stories

Drifting North...1

The Oak Grove..3

Culture Shock...5

Stormy Weather 6

Tuatha Dé Danann...7

Summer Trilogy 8

Faith 9

Small Worlds 10

At The Duke with Five Days to Go..12

Awake 13

Darkness..14

Basic Grammar 16

The Last King of Ulster..18

Boys 20

This Dark 21

A Long Wednesday Night at Grianán an Aileach 22

The Best Things About Being Young in Derry..............................24

Watching Football 26

The Weight 29

30 January 1972..31

Peace 34

Summer Vacation 35

Daybreak 37

She's the Belle 39

Saviour..41

I Got Lost on the Way from Here to Bushmills 43

Ring...46

History Lesson 48

Storm 50

Night and Fog 52

Los San Patricios 54

The Morning After 56

For Owen Who Did Not Think Donegal Had Proper Beaches 57

In America 58

The Third Man 81

Priceless 83

Heat 85

Line of Sight 86

Walls 87

Daybreak 88

Borderline 90

Iarnóin 91

Flight 92

Justice 93

Easter 95

Skinnydipping in Ireland 97

Shelter 98

Poetry 99

Degrees of Damage 101

This Dublin Night 103

10 February 104

A History of Irish Dreams 105

The Border 108

Atlantic Dream 110

A History of the Bogside 111

An Encyclopedia of Saints 113

Peat 115

from Wikipedia

Derry or **Londonderry** (Irish: *Doire* or *Doire Cholm Chille*) is a city in Northern Ireland. The old walled city of Londonderry lies on the west bank of the River Foyle, and the present city now covers both banks (*Cityside* to the west and *Waterside* to the east) and is connected by two bridges. The district extends to rural areas to the southeast of the city. The population of the city proper was 83,652 in the 2001 Census. The *Derry Urban Area* had a population of 90,663, and is the second-largest city in Northern Ireland, the fourth on the island of Ireland. It is one of the only places in Europe not to have its walls breached. Derry is near the border with the Republic of Ireland. The district is run by Derry City Council and has an airport, City of Derry Airport, and a seaport, Londonderry Port.

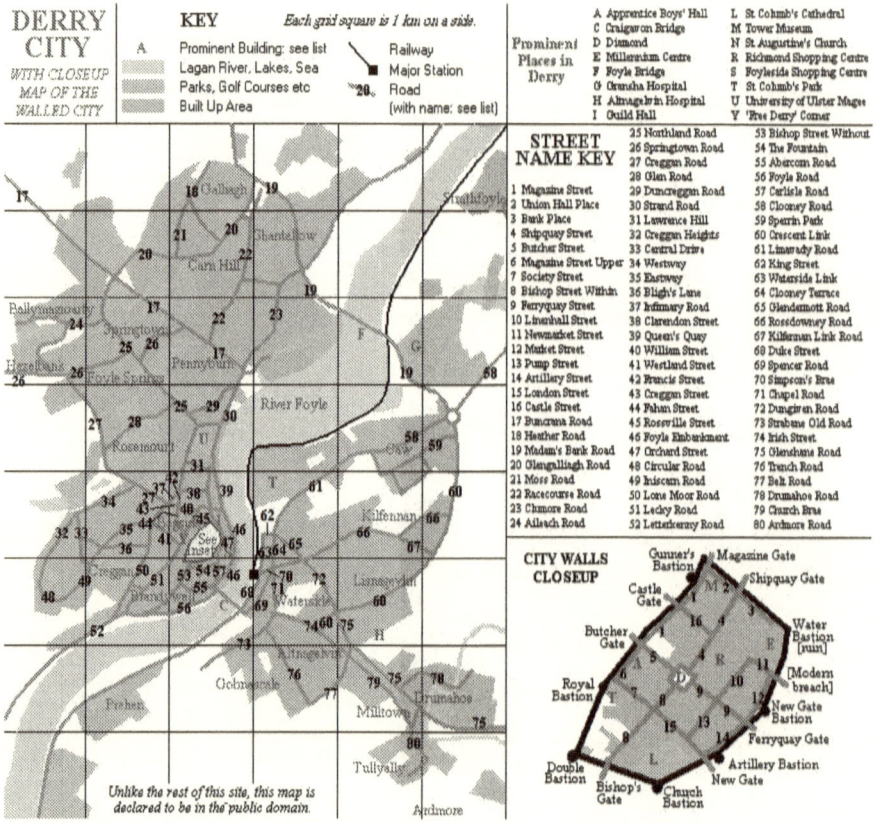

Ulster (Irish: *Cúige Uladh / Ulaidh*, Ulster Scots: *Ulstèr*, is one of the four traditional provinces of Ireland, in addition to Connaught, Munster and Leinster. Six of Ulster's nine counties, Antrim (*Aontroim*), Armagh (*Ard Mhacha*), Down (*An Dún*), Fermanagh (*Fear Manach*), Londonderry (*Doire*) (formerly known as County Coleraine before being renamed and expanded during the Plantation of Ulster) and Tyrone (*Tír Eoghain*), form

Northern Ireland, and remained part of the United Kingdom after the partition of Ireland in 1921. Three Ulster counties, Cavan (*An Cabhán*), Donegal (*Dún na nGall*) and Monaghan (*Muineachán*) form part of the Republic of Ireland. About half of Ulster's population lives in Counties Antrim and Down. Many inhabitants (especially unionists) refer to the six-county Northern Ireland as "Ulster".

Northern Ireland (Irish: *Tuaisceart Éireann*) is a part of the United Kingdom lying in the northeast of the island of Ireland, covering 5,459 square miles (14,139 km², about a sixth of the island's total area). As of the UK Census in April 2001, its population was 1,685,000, between a quarter and a third of the island's total population.

Northern Ireland consists of six of the nine counties of the province of Ulster. The remainder of the island of Ireland is a sovereign state, the Republic of Ireland.

Ireland (Irish: *Éire*), is a country in north-western Europe occupying five-sixths of the island of Ireland. It is bordered by Northern Ireland (part of the United Kingdom) to the north, by the Atlantic Ocean to the west and by the Irish Sea to the east. The term Republic of Ireland (Irish: *Poblacht na hÉireann*) is officially used as "the description of the State."

Ireland (Irish: *Éire*; Ulster Scots: *Airlann*) is the third largest island in Europe behind Great Britain and Iceland. It is also the twentieth largest in the world. It lies to the northwest of Continental Europe. It is surrounded by hundreds of islands and islets. To the east of Ireland, separated by the Irish Sea, is the island of Great Britain. Politically, the Republic of Ireland (also known simply as Ireland) covers five sixths of the island, with Northern Ireland, part of the United Kingdom, covering the remainder in the northeast. The name 'Ireland' derives from Old Irish Ériu (in modern Irish, *Éire*) with the addition of the Germanic word 'land'. This word, from Proto-Celtic, which also gave Middle Welsh *Iwerd* "Irish Sea", originally meant "fatness", in the sense of fertile.

The population of the island is slightly under six million (2006/7), with almost 4.25 million in the Republic of Ireland (1.7 million in Greater Dublin) and an estimated 1.75 million in Northern Ireland (0.6 million in Greater Belfast).

The Troubles (Irish: *Na Trioblóidí*) is a term used to describe the latest installment of periodic communal violence involving Republican and Loyalist paramilitary organisations, the Royal Ulster Constabulary (RUC), the British Army and others in Northern Ireland from the late 1960s until the Belfast Agreement of 10 April 1998. The Troubles have been variously described as terrorism, ethnic conflict, a many-sided conflict, a guerrilla war, a low intensity conflict, and even a civil war.

drifting north

This is way north, you understand. We're at fifty-five degrees north. Fifty-five! I mean, really. About where Moscow or the southern end of Hudson's Bay lie. South of Aberdeen sure, and Stockholm, and Helsinki, and St. Petersburg, and, what's the capitol of Norway? Whatever. But north of every major city in Canada. And so, even now in spring, early spring, sunrise is crossing the six in the morning barrier while sunset doesn't fall before nine in the evening, a fifteen hour day almost two months before the Summer Solstice.

Oslo. Yes, Oslo. Oslo is north of us as well. And Riga, and Copenhagen too.

That is not to say that we are a cold place. We are not. Northern Europe lives on that gift of the Caribbean, the Gulf Stream and the North Atlantic Drift, which stretch equatorial heat to our cold sea, warming the land, bringing copious rains, and huge harvests of fish.

In university I learned that Ireland itself has drifted north over the eons, and had fallen below the sea and risen again all through the history of creation. That coral reefs on an underwater tropical Ireland formed our limestone. And falling again into a turbulent chalky ocean covered this northern coast in its white stones. That sixty-five million years ago this spot of land drifted over a crack in the earth's crust and volcanoes pushed the black basalt up through the chalk. Then, fifty million years of rain wore our mountains down into the thick rich soil that pulled those ancient people across the turbulent waters to these shores.

"Everything takes time," Father Malachi would say often, as we sat in his classroom at St. Peter's. "Not even the Lord could build this world in a day."

This is way north. And in the warm seasons we have all day, very long days, to see where we are on this planet at this moment and to gaze at our far horizons and find where we are going. We are very lucky beings, I think, to live in a universe of movement: Our earth hurtles through space at almost thirty kilometers each second while spinning at over six hundred kilometers per hour, circling a sun that moves through an expanding universe. And on this planet we sit on mammoth plates of land that slide across the globe, surrounded by seas full of their own rivers of liquid movement. The hot center of our earth pushes us up, and the chill rains wear us down. The atmosphere flows around us without pause, warming us, cooling us, and pushing oxygen toward us.

Last night I felt trapped by the limits of time and space. I sat surrounded by walls and work and the world seemed cold and hard. Today I will stay outside, where the view of the future embraces me, sailing northward on this tiny green isle, through endless possibility.

The Oak Grove

The hills described how we ran. Down, from Creggan to the Bogside or along the outside of the walls down to the Foyle we raced with absolute abandon. You have to walk these hills, if you are a flatlander, to understand. And we had no shoes with rubber soles, just leather for school or our cleated football boots, and neither could offer any grip on the paving stones worn smooth from a century or more of traffic and rain. Up, back from the river and perhaps the soldiers, up to the fields where we'd play games, we charged, our legs pumping high, challenging gravity with every step.

Seven thousand years ago the first humans to see this river valley found the tall oak trees growing on an island in the center of a fish-filled river and knew it as a holy place. Fifteen hundred years ago St. Columba and his monks came and consecrated the spot. Four hundred years ago the English came and fortified their frontier fort and town against the dangerous and uncivilized natives. Eighty-five years ago Cumann na nGaedhael negotiators in London let the Brits keep this port and naval base just inside their separation line, despite an overwhelming Catholic and Republican majority. And thirty-five years ago British Paras shot down twenty-six people – killing fourteen – who had the nerve to ask for the right to vote and the right to trial in their own country. The streets we ran bled history. Today a Marks and Spencer and a Debenham's stand in the Foyleside Centre in one of those places we used to run. Is this our victory or the ultimate win for a new kind of colonialism?

We walk up the wall from the Ferryquay Gate to the Church Bastion, and look down the incredible angle at the two sides of these massive walls. And then we continue up to Bishop's Gate. Inside the wall the remnant of the Brit Army observation base stands forbidding and green and bristling with surveillance cameras. Outside, past Nailors Row, where long ago cobblers in tiny stone houses squeezed out a living fixing the boots of their overlords, all the old homes are gone – but Derry still looks like Derry. A little rough. A little dirty. A little old. A little poor.

Two unsupervised boys climb on a stand of newspapers outside a News Agent's shop, threatening to tip it over. My friend, who grew up safe and obedient in the American Midwest, laughs and asks if that scene might be familiar. I just laugh too. Down below us the river runs deep and grey and timeless. To the west the horizon marks the border, just above the cemetery that is oh so filled with loss. And there is the Bogside. All new housing but the same in so many ways. Behind us is a city center rebuilding, resurgent, re-imagined, where hotels like the City and the Tower will charge you two hundred American dollars for a room for a night in this place that was the Fallujah of the 1970s.

The boys finally topple the stand, and laugh, and run, as the merchant rushes out cursing: the rich northern version of "fuck" repeated a hundred times. And now I laugh too. The night before I had dwelt on Seamus Heaney's words: "My heart besieged by anger, my mind a gap of danger, I walked among their old haunts, the home ground where they bled; And in the dirt lay justice like an acorn in the winter, Till its oak would sprout in Derry where the thirteen men lay dead." But perhaps the ghosts matter less now. "Let's leg it," I shout, a phrase she does not understand, so I grab her hand, and pull her along, and we run down the hill, and twist through an alley, and race down a winding street falling at more than thirty degrees, and spill out onto the wide grass bank that separates the walls from the Bogside, and fall and roll together, breathless and out of control, laughing and laughing.

We sit on the lawn at the edge of footwalk, our breathing recovering, and I pick grass from her hair. Back then, in the late afternoons, as the dangerous dark approached, we would have been sitting in the shadow of the Rossville Flats and surrounded by barbed wire – theirs and ours. "Do you love this place?" I ask. "It is fascinating," she says diplomatically, "and it is who you are, so I'm grabbing all I can." I quote a different Heaney poem, "and smile, As you find a rhythm, Working you, slow mile by mile, Into your proper haunt, Somewhere, well out, beyond..." "What are you talking about?" she asks. "Nothing really, where's the car?" "Back up at the top." "Aye," I say.

culture shock

At half eight in the rain the couple behind us on Baggot Street is in distress. "Oh," she yells, "There! It says 'late night pharmacy!'" – which indeed it does – on the sign – but, of course, the shop is closed and dark. He looks at his wrist, "What does "late night" mean here, it's eight-thirty?" "Late night means six or half past," I offer, "except maybe in the city centre, but there is a Tesco right over there for things." "They don't have sleeping pills," the woman whines. "We just got in from L.A. and I can't sleep and it's cold and wet." "Have a pint," I suggest, "or a whisky, and climb under your duvet, and you will sleep. As for the rest, we've been complaining 'bout the weather for a few thousand years, and nothing seems to help." The California man looks at me with the full bore of colonial disgust. I just smile as we walk away, down to the next pub.

stormy weather

It was a snow for the ages. We had to get up to the oldest grandparents to find something that matched. "Not since twenty-three laddy, and then we could barely get out of the house for a week." The city stopped in its tracks. Silence descended. The white curtain was so thick that even our childhood shouts became lost in the wind-twisted folds. We ran down the hill to the river and by the time we ran back up every one of our footprints had disappeared. Our parents, who in the morning had tried to fight the storm with shovels and brooms, gave up and retreated to their warm kitchens. The constabulary vanished, unable to get their cars through the drifts. The soldiers must have gone back to their barracks for tea. Dirty, dangerous Derry became a glimmering city of children at play.

I stepped away from the group for a moment. It was only a few yards but it left me in a funnel of spinning white. I heard nothing but the gentle clatter of snowflake against snowflake. It was the quietest and safest thing I had known in two years.

Then Katherine burst in, "There you are," she said, "I got worried." Only her reddened face was in colour, everything else was covered in the frost. Sometimes the only thing safer than your own space is the smile of someone caring. "Back up to the top," I yelled, "Let's leg it all the way to the school ground." And off we raced through the cloud.

Tuatha Dé Danann

In the legends our ancient race of gods now hides underground – waiting. Waiting to be invoked to the grand cause; and then they will arise and fight alongside us mortals.

"Do you ever lose the fantasy world?" she asks. Above us clouds have filled the sky, except for a deep pool of black where Leo the Lion of the Night-Sky sits looking down at us. As a child I knew that the lion represented England and asked my Da if there was a constellation of the harp. He laughed softly, lit another cigarette, and told me to find that one for myself.

"Why would I lose it?" I ask in return. "The real world is hard enough even with my escapes." And she laughs.

Around the fire we learned that when Tuatha Dé Danann joined the fight they would be invisible, but armed with lances of blue flame and shields of pure white. "So you can see the lances and the shields but not the fighters?" my trouble-causing brother had asked. The adults all smiled at the question, but gave no answer.

"That happened here," I tell her, "and five thousand years before that, Dagda, the king of Tuatha Dé Danann built a fort here from where you can see more than half of Ulster, and fifteen hundred years ago the Uí Neill, the High Kings of Ulster, stood here and surveyed their empire. And sometime after that, Eogháin was baptised here by St. Patrick himself. And five hundred years after that, somebody built these walls."

"And somehow," she says, "you can walk through all that, can't you." There is no question. I can. The ancient ring forts filled with myths are my place to retreat to, no matter where I spend a night.

"Now I know where you are as you fall asleep," she tells me. "I have been wondering." "They'll come back you know," I say, looking at her and the sweep of the dark lough beyond. "They will come back, invisible with fiery swords and brilliant shields. They will come back and make all things right."

And she just smiles once more.

summer trilogy

One

To get there required so much. We could catch the Donegal coach as far as Clady. The older people always talked of taking the Great Northern Railway on this route, but all that was left by our time were a few rusting rails along overgrown gravel paths that led to stations sitting in pointless wait. So it was the coach that left from the stop above the bridge and then we got off at Clady and walked or begged lifts through Kennystown and Glentimon, Victoria Bridge and Erganagh, Castlederg and Castlegore, Killen and Carrickcroghery, Tonwore and Drumbrick, Kesh and Letterkeen and Drumrush, until we'd finally step on the eastern bridge to Boa Island. It took many hours, sometimes a day. That summer we crossed that edge of Lower Lough Erne just before the sun came up, and stopped to eat cold sausage and brown bread at the old cemetery, watched by the figures of the most ancient gods. Then we couldn't wait any longer, and took the first path on our left, and raced to the shore, stripping naked, diving into the water, and not coming out until the sun stood atop the sky.

Two

The summer heat had risen from the south chasing the cool ocean breezes away and we needed to get out of the city but, moving north or east involved risks not consistent with the romance of the moment so we went south, staying inside the winding path of the borderline, until we felt that we had slipped the constraints of time and the rules of nations. The bridge was ancient. The fields a stunning green. The sheep sounded in the distance. The river spoke of a history reaching back to the very beginnings. We spread our blanket there, dipped our feet into the cooling water. And then made love embraced by the soft haze of the late afternoon.

Three

We got lost among the ruins in the cool damp. Somewhere above us the sky was ablaze with a noontime August sun, but here the stones were cold, and the colour so deep, and all routes simply a tangle of expectation and memory. "I wished I lived back when there were knights and stuff," he said, "stead of now, when there's shite." The rest of us could not argue. So, instead of searching for a path out, we climbed deeper in, hoping we could discover a gateway filled with enough magic.

---

faith

The grandfathers told us the stories. There were the swirls of peat smoke and the thickness of rough pipe tobacco and harsh breaths from British cigarettes and voices that carried a history of unfathomable length in their soft depths. There was no line between myth and history, as is probably the correct thing, and so the Fianna ghost warriors who would sweep the English out of Derry and the visions of St. Patrick chasing the snakes and the Flight of the Earls and the kings of Tara and the victories over the Vikings and risings of 1798 and 1916 were all one story that I and every other child in Derry knew more fully than any catechism.

I was raised to believe in magical swords and saints riding to the rescue and with the knowledge that the very earth of our country was so nurturing that it could be burned to warm us on the cold, wet days. I still believe in all of that.

And I learned to believe in the Holy Catholic Church. In confession. In communion. I have no doubt that when I receive communion the body of Jesus is joined to me. I have no doubt that his blood is there, purifying my own, trying to save me. I have no doubt that Jesus died on the cross for our sins. And I am genuinely sorry that we have not made better use of that gift.

And I learned to believe in the struggle. In the fight against evil in the abused the land of my birth. The IRA was Pádraic Pearse and Michael Collins. The IRA had freed most of the island and made us a nation again. And perhaps that the new IRA would free the rest of us if we could be, if nothing else, absolutely silent when we needed to be.

It was an unquestioned Holy Trinity. God and magic and human struggle. And I could sit in the church in the late morning of any Sunday and let the stories in the glass windows and the words of the priest and those voices that reached out from the ancient stones all wash over me, holding this otherwise slippery world, temporarily constant.

small worlds

The old black Humber Hawk would wake all of us with its cough as it tried to start in the hour before dawn on Tuesdays and Thursdays. It was the only car on the street. It was the only car for many streets back then and if any of us lads had ever been in an automobile it was either this one or maybe, if you'd been caught, an RUC car.

Aedan's grandfather worked for the Bishop. He went to Belfast on those mornings for the church and came back late in the evenings. We had no idea what he might have been doing there. Belfast was impossibly far away. Only Aedan had been there and he talked about how big it was and how the giant cranes towered over the shipyards. "They built the Titanic there," he told us, "I saw where. It was the biggest ship ever but it hit an iceberg and sank and everyone died." This was an amazing story. We argued about when it might have happened. "Long back." "Very long?" "Before the war." "In the war the Germans sank a lot of boats with torpedoes." We knew this. There were uncles and grandfathers lost on those Royal Merchant Ships – even on American ships. But before the war? "Maybe 1938 or like that," Aedan said. That seemed possible. An iceberg! Eventually someone would have to ask an adult.

Seamus had been to Dublin. Out of the twenty of us that ran these streets he was the only one. He had an uncle there. He told us it was "biggest city in the world except for London and New York." Rian challenged that. "Paris is bigger, and Tokyo." But that did not seem possible. We had never seen a French person, how many could there be? And we only knew people from Asia from American war movies, we were hardly sure that Tokyo was more real than Oz or Narnia.

Thomas and I and others had been in Donegal. Thomas and I had been all the way to the sea where we could look west to that New World and all that it promised. Trevor had spent a week somewhere near Coleraine when a rich cousin had come from Chicago. They had taken him to see the Giant's Causeway on a coach. He had told us that so long ago – so, so long back before Wolfe Tone even – when people were much bigger, you could walk to Scotland on those stones in the ocean. "Is that how the Proddies got over here?" Kelvin asked. "No you gobshite," Thomas said, "They came on boats and cut off their hands and threw them here. That's why they've got that on their flag." Thomas was very smart. We knew that. So somehow this was accepted without argument.

We would tell these stories over and over. Long into the night. Even at that young age. Though when we heard the old black Humber Hawk rumbling over the pavers, and would spot its wavering headlamps, we would know it was time to head toward our beds.

at The Duke with five days to go

She rang me as I was driving back from Belfast and said, "Can you come by on your way?" And I was battling to stay awake as I moved south through the fog, but said, "Absolutely, I'll see you then," and we talked for 15 minutes or so and then clicked off and I switched from listening to RTE Lyric to BBC 2 hoping conversations would keep me awake – then started jumping through CDs because that was not solving the problem – and before I got two songs into a road mix of The Stones, Dylan, and random Irish crap, she rang again.

"I've got to get out," she said this time. "Can'ya meet at The Duke?" "I have to park the car down there?" I was momentarily whining. "Stop, it'll be late, and just one pint" "Yeah, it'll be late, but sure." "Ring when you get to the city." "When I pass the airport." "Just, anyway, thanks." "Soright," I say in my best American cartoon voice, and click off again and start singing along to *Tumbling Dice.*

We sat outside. It was colder than it should have been, but that just left us in the quiet. The sky was crystal, and even here, just off Grafton Street, we could see stars flashing from the heavens. I told her to get some kind of *Sex and the City* drink, but she just went with St. Brendan's and coffee. I went for whisky and Smithwicks and coffee to make it look like I was willing to stay up, because, tired as I was, I was. "Are we really OK?" her voice the softest note on the empty street. "I mean, the house, us together, you're not over-whelmed, are you? You think it will all work?" I took her hands under the table. And then I just held them. "Everything is a little scary, but everything good should be, I'm just completely excited." She trembled but smiled. "Really," I said. "Really."

Her grip tightened but her muscles softened. "I just got frightened, sitting and packing alone tonight." "You should be frightened of moving in with someone like me." "You're just trying to make me laugh." "Yes, I am." "So we're really OK?" The waitress has reappeared. In her soft Cork accent she asks, "Need anything?" "She needs reassurance that I'm not dangerously insane," I say, "so we can live together happily ever after." The waitress looks at me. Looks at her. Looks back at me. "Looks completely mental to me," she says, "But you're the American girl who's ended up with a northern boy. So you might want to run lassie." And she turns and walks away.

I smile, but neither of us is looking at the waitress anymore.

awake

When I was but seven there was a broken wall three blocks from home where they were tearing the old houses down to build the new and I would sneak out and walk there in the hours before the sun rose and climb up and lie facing the sky as it turned from deep grey to lighter grey or from star-flecked night to the pale blue of the first of morning or once, when I was luckiest, from the dance of the northern lights to a fiery red dawn. Then I would go back home chilled but more certain that the earth would stay on course.

darkness

There are many ways in which the world divides, and one is this. There are those who, as children, have lived in places where disturbing sounds in the night turn lights on and bring people to windows and doors. And there are those who, as children, have lived in places where those sounds engender darkness and silence and invisibility.

When I am back home I walk up the hill from the Foyle. Everything has changed. Everything is different. The dim and tiny terrace homes that had stood for centuries to hold the overcrowded families of the Catholic lower class have disappeared, first swapped for the horrors of sixties and seventies urban rebuilding, places like the highrise Rossville Flats, and then again for the colourful stucco of the homes that today line these streets. Now there are real furnaces and real water heaters and good plumbing and they do not tilt the way the old ones did. The roofs and windows truly keep out the rain and the North Atlantic wind, and new smaller families fit comfortably in new larger bedrooms.

But none of that is important. Because I tend to see what was there. Between the sky and the paving stones my eyes and ears fill with phantoms. If it is daylight children run down streets laughing as grim-faced soldiers hold automatic rifles. If it is night then the demons run wild, no matter what I try to do. In those nights every shot, every wrong footfall, every yell, every heavy vehicle tyre sound – and all these came with every sunset – were greeted by people shutting lamps off, and drawing curtains, and shushing children, and keeping them out of the range of windows and doors.

And there is nothing more frightening to a child than to see fear in their parents' eyes.

So yesterday I sat at a dinner table, and was introduced to a compatriot, as she called herself, or another expatriate, I wanted to counter, but attempting politeness – chose not to. "From what I hear," she said, "you must be delighted by the breakthroughs this weekend. Now things can really start to be over." She was, I had learned, Protestant, from Hillsborough, the big-treed, high-tea, old "Royal Suburb" south of Belfast, but had lived in West London for the last 20 years. Life in nice places – I thought – must be wonderful, and you cannot really hold it against them. "I suppose," I offered, "it suggests a chance, and a chance is better than what we have had." I shifted my speech to sound as fully a Derry Catholic as possible. That sound a Dublin friend calls "Irritable Vowel Syndrome." "You wouldn't be one of those Sinn Fein hard-liners now would'ya?" She put on her imitation of a south Dublin accent to say this – pushing me just a bit more. But I breathed in deeply, and exhaled slowly. "Nah," I said, "the other end of the spectrum. John Hume was a friend of my Da's. I've always been on the side of the angels. And like all angels, I'm just waiting for humanity to understand."

basic grammar

In Irish, and especially in the deeply antiquated Ulster form, you are not "sick" or "well" or "happy" or "sad." You may "exist as sick" - "Gan a bheith ar do chóir féin," or you might "perceive yourself as unwell," - "Aireachtáil rud beag tinn," but it is not the absolute state implied by the grammar of English. Possessions, similarly, are simply your's by proximity, "Tá airgead agam" – "there is money at me." It is a language of people who know that very little is permanent.

We have awakened early, and have entered Tesco before both crowds or most daily items arrive. But we assemble beers and cheeses, meats and the very last loaf of brown bread in the aisle, smoked salmon and plastic utensils. Without asking I toss a variety of sweets and cakes into the trolley, those unhealthiest of childhood desires. At the counter she picks these up. "Jammie Dodgers?" "They're just 46 pence." "Oh, that would be an excuse... and, mini Jaffa Cakes?" "Breakfast of champions." "What are you? Still ten?" "I can be an adult when I must be." Perhaps that is not exactly the answer that she wishes. Perhaps.

We drive east towards the beach I want us to be at. We both drink coffee. She spoons yogurt into her mouth, and I push cakes into mine. *The White Album* plays on the CD, "When you find yourself in the thick of it / Help yourself to a bit of what's all around you / Silly girl. / Martha my dear you have always been / My inspiration / Please / Be good to me Martha my love." I sing along. "Where I come from boys didn't sing much," she says, "except maybe in church." "Is that not masculine in America?" "I think they sing with each other, less when girls are around." "They make great music in the states," I tell her, "but it is not a musical culture. I always thought it would be, 'cause of the old movies and all, but it really is not." "It is a literal place – we have fewer fantasies." "Yeah," and I say this with deep regret.

Everything about her childhood is so different than mine. That rock-ribbed Calvinist Republican upbringing in a tiny monoculture east of Lake Michigan, the quiet church-run schools, the lack of conflict in family and community, the lack of travel, the lack of danger. Her very words are not the same: "religion" has a different definition, so does "history," so does "freedom," and so does "family." "Home," I know, means something clear and stable to her, it stands almost just as she left it, on a street named after a bird in a neighborhood filled with streets named after birds, it is one story with a paneled family room in the basement, it occupies a large green and flat swath that must be watered all summer because the only grass native to that region are tall dune grasses. Her mom and dad are still there, the furniture has changed but the arrangement has not. There is still church every Sunday morning and the same circle of friends. "Home" to me is a concept, a memory, a fragment of a song recalled as I fall asleep. I tell people that my Ma sang me to sleep with Clapton's *White Room* but that is an obvious lie. Yet, yes, if you say "home," it is music that comes to me, or the smells of mash or boxty or turf burning on the grate or my father's cigarettes, or just the way rain sounded on that roof so long ago demolished to make way for "decent housing." Do we mean the same thing when we say "love"?

I do not ask this question. I have always been afraid of unknown answers. I am not a brave person by nature, only by pretense. Instead I smile and we pass Portrush and head toward the White Rocks when the whole beach will be ours alone. "You might not feel it now / But when the pain cuts through you're going to know, and how. / The sweat is gonna fill your head, / When it becomes too much you'll shout aloud, / But you'll have to have them all pulled out after the Savoy truffle," The Beatles sing, and I sing along.

We are a musical people. A poetic people. We hide behind our words and our melodies. This might keep the world at a distance from which we can focus on it, or it just may allow enough space for us to see what we wish to see.

The Last King of Ulster

The telephones rang in the night and the men were told that they might come and get James from hospital at the dawn, when the curfews for Catholics ended. And so six of them – carefully chosen to avoid trouble - went with the first light in Keegan's coughing old Rover, past the barricades, out of the "No Go Zone," and through the Brit checkpoints. They brought him back an hour past, looking like a mummy. And we stood in the street in silence. And many swore vengeance.

No kid in the entire northwest was better at hurling than James. No one. The hurley had seemed just a part of his body since he had been a wee lad – and he was fast. Storm-fucking wind fast as they say, and so coveted by the GAA football coaches and the soccer football coaches and everyone who worked in athletics – but all he wanted to play at was this ancient game.

Einstein said the gravity was not really a pulling force in the way old Isaac Newton said and the rest of us think. He said objects in motion bend the fabric of time and space and other objects tend to follow in those creases. My memories of James racing the length of the pitch at this GAA ground or that make that idea obvious to me now. When I close my eyes I can see him bend the turf to his game, and I can watch all the other players follow despite their best intentions.

Sure, you say, especially if you would be from Antrim or Down or Armagh – but hurling is not much in Derry or Donegal. Those other counties are GAA counties, and the hurling and the football are the biggest games among the Catholics. While Derry is the one place in the north where Football, the soccer kind, is more popular with Catholics than the old Gaelic games. There is not the fight between "English" and "native" games here, that is true. Yet none of that changes a thing. Even in games against the best clubs from Antrim, even against those clubs when the lads from Derry would be beaten badly, the matches still revolved around James, with three or four of their backs doing not a thing but falling into his orbit, swinging their sticks in vague hopes of hooking the sliotar from him.

But all that was from the before time. And then the teams could not travel, not to the Republic because of the border, and surely not elsewhere within the Province because you could easily be killed, and though soccer went on up at the school field in Creggan, and a little Gaelic football went on at the club, James could do little more than toss the sliotar back and forth with a few other lads. Though, in the early morning, you might see him running through the cemetery on the hill, twisting and turning among the stones, all while keeping that small ball on that flat stick. And if the light was right, the dead of Derry seemed as pulled to him as his live opponents had been.

And then, in one of the riots, while the other boys were throwing the stones of the old demolished houses at the Army, James suddenly rose on the rock pile and in one brilliant move swatted the sliotar at the Paras with the perfection of his greatest scoring strike, striking a soldier directly in the face mask, shattering it. And in this moment he became our Cuchulainn, our reincarnation of the Hound of Ulster, the boy hurler born of a god who defended the homeland when it mattered the most.

A fortnight later the Paras lifted him off the street, and he vanished into the lost world of British authority.

When the men brought him back six weeks after that his legs and arms were broken and his skull was cracked and there were tales of burn marks on his body in places no one would want burn marks.

His body did heal. But from then on he was very quiet, and he did not run anymore.

He is old now. I am getting there and he had at least a decade on me, if I remember correctly. And he works the bar at a quiet pub in Ballybofey, up in Donegal on the River Finn. He would not remember me. I was simply one of the wee lads, one of his fans. But I know him as soon as my eyes adjust to the dim after I walk in the door. And I smile as I did at five or six or seven as I watched him bend the world to his speed and power.

He draws the Guinness with barely a nod, while I look past him out a side window. The GAA stadium rises just beyond those trees. If I listen carefully, I can hear the yells of boys, and the smack of hurleys striking the sliotar.

boys (five more very short stories)

"She decided to try other things," he said. "Fuck," I said. "Yeah," he answered. "Let's go sit over there," he said, "We can see the match better." We switched tables. Liverpool still hadn't scored. "You'd think one of 'em could bounce a shot in off Crouch's head," I offered. "I'll spend less money if I'm single," he told me. "Yeah," I said.

His rank and name was "Colonel Sanders," which largely explained his decision to pursue assignments outside of the United States proper, but now he was not happy. Here in Algiers people did not meet him and immediately make jokes, but after years in Europe he found himself isolated by an inability to comprehend Arabic and sorrowed by the loss of a woman left behind in Kaiserslautern. He would not share information at first. He had grown up in the American South and distrusted cops and New Yorkers. But I spoke English and after three evenings of conversation, beers, and absinthe among the elaborate mosaics of the El Djazair Hotel Bar, I was offered what I needed.

I met him Tuesday on the bridge over the pond in St. Stephen's Green and he lit two joints as if he was Bogart lighting cigarettes for himself and Bacall – and handed one to me. A few years ago, getting high in the forecourt of The Market Bar, he had explained that the trick to not getting caught was not passing the illicit fags back and forth. This had proved true, at least as far as we had experienced. His friendship went back as far as I could recall, as did our ability to lead each other astray.

Andrew was already hammered in the pseudo-chic atmosphere of Pravda when I spotted him as I raced from a lunch meet with American students in Temple Bar north to Penney's to get something I had promised I'd pick up while "in the city." Even for him it was too early. He would not talk, but I sat next to him for the next five hours, assuring him he was not alone. When I finally bundled him in to a taxi and sent him home, Penney's was closed.

He was just sitting on the James Joyce Bridge, late, very late, there among the glow of post-modern architecture, and I had nowhere else to be, so I sat down and he began to tell stories. Some were ancient, some were inconceivable, others all too real, but I listened for hours. Then I gave him two two-Euro coins, and walked off into the pre-dawn fog, wishing we had all-night pubs here.

This Dark

My uncle Caolán disappeared off the street near Bishop's Gate and into Long Kesh on a fog enshrouded Saturday a fortnight fore Bloody Sunday back in Seventy-Two and we did not see him again til Seventy-Four. That was the way back then and there was not a thing anyone could do. So the families moved in together, crowding the house on St. Patrick Street, which now had to fit three adults, five lads and four girls. Aunt Onóra slept in the front room downstairs, on a day bed opposite the window, under the painting of a ship riding the rough Atlantic. The girls crowded into bunks in the upstairs front, the three younger boys shared an alcove at the top of the stairs, and Niall and myself dragged our blankets into the airless attic and lay beneath the rafters wishing for nightly rains that would drown our conversations before they drifted into the rooms below.

By but the light of a small oil lamp and the glowing ends of cigarettes – Players lifted from the table near where Onóra slept or joints rolled in single-handed elegance by Niall who told all that he had learned the technique so he need not stop wanking when he needed to get high – the two of us would plan all things, from stealing a fishing boat and sailing to Canada to blowing up the Brit watchtowers, from stowing away on the ferries to France to hiking to Galway and finding ladies. Dreams violent and dreams of escape and dreams of love. The stuff of boys.

I told him that I wanted to sail not to Canada but to St. Pierre off the coast, where we would be free and surrounded by both French women and the ocean. He told me that only an ijiot Irish fool would want to trade one cold island for another. He thought Australia might be the place to go. I said that was too far and honestly that I doubted the wisdom of running away only to end up on the bottom of the earth.

Below us our sisters spoke of boys and school and girls who might be "looking to find themselves in trouble." Our brothers talked of football and throwing rocks. My parents whispered that money was bitterly scarce and of their fears of the nightmares which would next take place. From the street came the sly steps of Provos running and deep vibrations of Brit armor patrolling and the clockwork bells of the churches. We could not hear Onóra who, like ourselves, sat smoking in the dark, with no certainty at'all of what might come with the dawn.

A Long Wednesday Night at Grianán an Aileach

It is a moment to tell stories, so I take him to the storytelling place. On an afternoon filled with the brightest sunshine we load the rumbling old Seat and drive out of the city, heading west along the N13.

Near Burt we turn off and head toward the ring fort. In the legends it was built almost nine thousand years ago, at least the earthen base, and the man-gods who had come from across the sea watched over both their earthly domains and the stars of their heavens from this promontory. We climb up in the warmth of the sun, just as the High King Daghda of the Tuatha Dé Danann did at the birth of the Celtic world. Others are about. Tourists. A few from down south. A few Americans. Five Chinese taking hundreds of photographs. A French couple far more interested in each other. But the site is vast, and we can share. Later they will leave, but we will not.

You can see seven of Ulster's nine counties from here. That's what the legends always said. All but Armagh and Down visible from this summit. Modern mapping has proved that to be true. Modern archaeology has shown the site to be all those nine thousand years old. What other truths, we need to ask, lie among the myths of the ancient poetry?

Bai ri amra for Eirinn do Thuathaib De a chenel, Eochaid Ollathar a ainm. Ainm n-aill do dano an Dagda, ar ba hé dognith na firta conmidhedh na sina na toirthe doib. Ba head asbeirdis combo dé asberthe Dagda fris. Bai ben la hEalcmar an Broga .i. Eithni a hainm. Ainm n-aill di Boand. Atacobair an Dagda dó a cairdeas collaidi. Aroét an ben ondon Dagda acht nibad oman Ealcmaire, ar med a chumachtai. Faidis an Dagda iarum Ealcmar n-uad for turus co Bres mac nEalathan co Mag nInis, 'ninais' dogeine an Dagda tincheadla mora for Ealcmar oc dul nuad, cona tisad i fairthi .i. a muichi, diuchtraisr díthrachtais gl. dithrachta .i. dealbha nó cur dorcha n-aidchi aire, argart gortai itaid de. Dobert imorchorafirst or i. mearaighthe H. mora fair, co torchaidh .ix. misa fri haenla. Fo bhith, asbertsom conicfad ider lá aidchi dia thig afrithisi. Luid an Dagda co mnai nEalcmair coléig co mac dó .i. Aengus a ainm, ba slan an bean dia galar ar cind Ealcmair, nir airigistairráthaigh fuirri a bine .i. teacht a coibligi an Dagdai.

He is sixteen now, and we are here. For a year? or two? or more. And he is at that age where the questions flow. But some answers do not belong in the air of the house. They need bigger places. They need the hills and the heavens. And so we walk this hill. We walk these two thousand year old stone fortifications. We talk about the small stuff. And we wait for night, and the constellations, and we wait to be alone.

When the sun sets and the glens below us fill with fogs and spirits, we light a candle in a glass jar and sit with our backs against the wall, under the protection of Pegasus, who paws at the roof of the universe.

And he asks about my brothers, and I tell him what I know. And he asks about his uncle, and I do the same. We pause. Eat sandwiches of cold black pudding and sharp cheese on black bread and wash them down with Smithwicks. And we stare off to the west, where the world is lost to the ocean.

And then he asks about me. He asks about the time between the Battle of the Bogside and the family flight to America. And he asks about the times afterwards when I came back. It has become important to him. It is not who he is, or who he will be, but it is the clay from which he has been formed.

I light two more candles. A trinity is important right now. And then I tell stories. There is chaos and violence. Fear and courage. Great joy and great misery. And I try to add just enough magic to cover for things unsaid.

"Is that all true?" he asks. It is now very late. We have moved to blankets on the grass, where we lie side by side, staring straight into the sky, straight into the past, straight back towards the creation itself. "As far as I can tell it," I say. "All of our stories are as true as we know how to tell them."

He closes his eyes. "If how you can tell it changes, will you tell me?" "It is always changing," I tell my child, "and certainly, you will be the first to know."

The Best Things About Being Young in Derry

If you could'a grown up so close to the swiftest flowing river in Europe, I'd bet you would'a wanted to. Not just because the current rushes past toward the lough and the sea, a swirling deep blue wonder, but because that speed made this magical valley in the ancient stone hills, a valley lit by the golden sunrises of that begin when the sun climbs beyond Scotland and by the multi-coloured light shows of the North Atlantic sunsets. A valley that lies under the most majestic rolling cloudbanks in the rain and a sweep of blue I have seen nowhere else on this planet when our local star shines through. A valley filled with mists in the night that carry the ghosts of nine millennia of history, and which opens into a spectacular bay surrounded by haunted highland shores.

Have people lived in your town for 9,000 years? The same culture? Nah, I didn'a think so. Unless you're from Baghdad or something. Then, OK, you've probably got me.

Because we have the stories. We have the Tuatha Dé Danann who came from either Alba or the sky as the glaciers fell back and found, at the oak grove on the hill in the middle of the river, the perfect place suspended between the heaven and the earth. And we have Cúchulainn defending Ulster (even if we had to move him a bit westward for our purposes), and we have the Fenians whose ghosts still walk the dales west of us, and whose flaming swords still lie buried beneath the soft sod, awaiting the moment when liberation will come.

Not even Dublin's got all that.

And for telling those stories we have the turf fires. The slow smoldering, faintly glowing warmth that we can sit around as we are enveloped in the smoke. The burning peat creates our own world, where all of this becomes not just possible, but surely true. And within that circle of smoke, we have the best storytellers, the Seanchaidh, the one's who carry the tales. That is a craft passed down from generation to generation, going all the way back. It is how we know exactly who we are.

They can talk down south, of course, but they cannot tell these stories the way we do, and the other nations, they are too young. They all came after the Celts, long after, so they can'na remember when the gods and giants strode the earth.

Then there are the walls. Oh yes, I know. They symbolise much that is terrible, but they are magnificent despite it all. They are so thick, and so strong, so solid and so old, and just so beautiful as a thing rising above your view as you play on an afternoon street. Most places, I have since learned, do not have 400 year old walls surrounding the city centre. They do not. I think, perhaps at age eight, I assumed that everyone had this. But then you learn just how lucky you are.

And when we could go west or east, into Donegal or up to the north coast. To the most ancient sites of Inishowen or the most gorgeous beaches spreading beneath the chalk cliffs, we knew we lived in a place blessed by God with so much more than its share of beauty, so much more than its share of wonder...

But mostly it was the people. I've loved many places. New York is the world's greatest city, filled with the world's best people. Parisians have won my heart many times. Rome is a wonder, an absolute wonder, not because of the ruins or the Cathedrals, but because of the joy. And Dublin, well, yes, Dublin - it is civilisation the way it was meant to be. But in Derry there was never one moment of doubt about what truly mattered, nor about how anyone would do anything they could to help, nor about the idea that everyone you met was looking out for you in every way. We were wrapped in a cocoon of humanity that loved us. No kid could ever ask for anything more.

Watching Football

The pub is full, though, surely, it always would be at this hour, and it holds all ages, as it usually does. Peadar in the corner by the window might be ninety. Michael's son Micky has his son Michael sitting in his lap, and little Michael isn't quite eight weeks. There are the kids I grew up with, and many of their parents, and more of the children of my friends, and grandchildren. The table with the five elderly women that sits under the telly and thus out of its view, includes the lavender smelling nurse who once helped set my broken leg when I was but nine. Seven of my youngest brother's old school boys crowd around one high table near the dart boards. It is absolutely like being home.

The televisions are all tuned to the Champions League match and we are all cheering for Liverpool. Of course. Oh, sure, there are kids on the street with Chelsea jerseys these days, even here. Like Yankee fans in America, paid-in-full success often sucks in the weak of heart. There's even a big rack of Chelsea gear at the JJB store in the Richmond Centre, across from the giant walls celebrating Scotland's great teams, Celtic and Rangers. The inventory, though, and the "25% off" signs, suggests that far more Liverpool, Arsenal, and Manchester United shirts have been sold this year. It should not be easy for any Irish to root for a club from the richest end of West London with a billionaire Russian owner. And anyway, Liverpool is part of us, is it not?

Not that Liverpool is the Catholic team in that town. It is not. Everton is, though that English city's sports scene has never developed the circus of sectarian hate that splits Glasgow apart for the profit of club owners.

But Liverpool is an Irish city. It is a first city of the diaspora, along with New York and Boston and Chicago. Hungry and abused, our ancestors fled for jobs and possibilities across the sea. To Liverpool to build ships. To New York and Chicago to build railroads. To Boston to harvest the timber of Maine and the fish of the Grand Banks. They were treated terribly in those places, but still, it was better, and still, they missed their home.

In the pub the smoke from the turf fire clouds the floor and the drinking is heavy, but in that Irish way. You cannot drink pints of Irish beers too fast. Surely not Guinness, but even Smithwicks and Harp go down more slowly. And plenty are not drinking alcohol. Kids slurp through Club Orange, and there are many tea pots and coffee cups on the tables. I'm soaking up my beer with a boxty which holds all the memories of the meals my Ma would serve in our tiny kitchen after my matches as a child on the club teams.

Sport is a kind of proxy warfare, right? And even with rich, crazy American owners and international cast of athletes, Liverpool reminds us of our own experiences in a way Chelsea cannot. There is the ultimate Scouser, Steven Gerrard, the kind of wild, tough, and crazy kid who drives everyone insane but will walk through hell with you, holding your hand. There is big, clumsy Peter Crouch, the kid who takes all the jokes but keeps going. There is Robbie Fowler, the slightly faded wonder boy who left and came back home, and Steve Finnan, the authentic fighter truly from this side of the Irish Sea. They are rough and unpredictable and deeply frustrating, as are our lives. The blue guys from London? Their international superstars radiate the kind of arrogance that elite school boys do. Even when they lose they always claim to be "the better team," because those in power always like to assert even the superiority of choosing to do things badly.

Before my boxty is touched, Liverpool is ahead. Kids in red number eight jerseys jump up and down. But we need more. This is only one leg of the two game set, and the Reds lost the first tie 0-1 in the besotted Anglican confines of London's Stamford Bridge grounds. Again and again the Liverpool offense rushes forward and puts shots on goal, but, well, football is a cruel game, and that net only looks big if you are the keeper. Twice the ball even goes in, only to be called back for offsides. Chelsea players flop to the ground seeking penalty kicks. Even the breathing in the pub is now geared to the tension of the game.

The match goes into extra time. Parents and grandparents now trade off walking with the wee ones outside. You can see impatience in the eyes of some. It is a beautiful night, should we not be out in the glorious twilight? But we need to see completion. Just two years ago people wrote off Liverpool in the Champions' Final in Istanbul when they were down three-nil, but they came back to win in penalties. No one wants to miss something like that.

I almost switch to coffee, but change my mind. Between the two halves of extra-time the boys in the back with instruments start playing, beginning with "Come out ye Black and Tans - come out and fight me like a man - show your wife how you won medals out in Flanders - tell her how the IRA made you run like hell away - from the green and lovely lanes in Killeshan-dra." which seems appropriate to the moment. Extra-time ends and the penalty-kick shootout begins.

I have watched and played football all of my life. I know that it is a waste of time, but I also know what the camaraderie brings. I've seen Derry when

Derry City has won, or even lost, like last year when they did not win in the UEFA Cup playing at Paris St. Germain in the Parc des Princes, a stadium so different in size and grandeur from the crumbling Brandywell that sits down the road from me now that it is almost inconceivable. I've seen the streets of Dublin when the Republic of Ireland has won big international matches. And just a few weeks ago I broke down and bought myself a Northern Ireland shirt on the morning after this little place had upended Sweden in European qualifying. We are tribal, we humans are, and this proxy warfare is far better than the alternative we have known too much of.

A friend brings another round and a thick plate of curry fries. And the room hushes with each kick, erupting after every Liverpool success. In just minutes it is over. Liverpool has won once again on an amazing goalkeeper performance. They are on their way to the Champions League Final in Athens. The musicians play "You'll Never Walk Alone," the Liverpool song, and half the room sings along, at least they sing as many words as they know. There is a lot of "dah, dah, dahing."

Then we all start to drift out into the night. It is still light, but the moon and the evening star glow overhead. The old nurse, with eyes and memory that I cannot fully understand, walks up to me and asks how my life has gone. Peadar asks if I can help him down the block and up the stairs. Michael says, "Stop by now for a nip of whiskey," and I assure him that I will.

I do walk Peadar to his flat. And I will go to Michael's. But between those moments I walk south. And I circle The Brandywell. The old grounds are deteriorating, but not in my eyes. I can still see the early 1960s, when every fan stood through every game, and the Candystripes took the double, and the world seemed a place full of invention and possibility, because we hadn't been taught different yet. The moonlight from the ever-darkening sky lights the stands that I can see, and somewhere high above a jet passes, adding the roar of the crowd.

I walk back past where I have come from. The music is drifting through the pub doors. "'Long time ago", said the fine old woman - "Long time ago", this proud old woman did say - "There was war and death, plundering and pillage - My children starved by mountain, valley and sea - And their wailing cries, they shook the very heavens - My four green fields ran red with their blood", said she..." I am in no mood for the sad songs of failed revolutions though. Not tonight. And I walk on toward Michael's. We will drink whiskey and break out the guitars and fiddles and sing better songs, ones from those Liverpool lads. "Love, love me do - You know I love you - I'll always be true - So please, love me do - Who-ho, love me do."

The Weight

Dropping out of the window as the Long Tower chimes three and clambering down the drainpipe I move slowly and do not jump so I can touch the pavers without a sound. The moon has me in its sights, a moving spotlight appearing in a gateway in the clouds, and the shadow is something fearful.

Keeping my shoes off I scurry in stockinged feet through the alleys, ears wide to the unique dangers of this summer. There is the depth of the rumble of the Brit APCs and the rhythmic beat of the boots of the Provos running and the sadder rhyme of the soldiers pounding their patrol routes. There is the silence of a city besieged and from the occasional open window the higher woodwind tones of mothers sobbing.

No one should be out on these streets right now, but all we have is each other and so I run to her when all pretend to sleep, and I run back when I have come to hope that this town's exhaustion has overtaken its fear and the people that surround me are truly at rest.

The street ahead has to be crossed and I lie face down on the cold stones, slipping forward, watching, listening. I feel the chill press through the fabric and shrink that Irish curse of mine – just a half hour ago it was filled and hot and wrapped in that tight love of hers – and I let myself know enough fear to keep me from the foolish bravery that has doomed us all.

Way off someplace. Way way off. There's a phonograph playing. I do not know why, but just now the streets are absorbing all of the bass notes, leaving only a treble voice scraping over the slate rooftops. "Go down, Miss Moses, there's nothin' you can say. It's just ol' Luke, and Luke's waitin' on the Judgement Day. Well, Luke, my friend, what about young Anna Lee? He said, 'Do me a favor, son, won't ya stay and keep Anna Lee company?'"

The voice pins me to the pavers. The moon is forcing hard shadows on the scene. The muscles in my chest are making it difficult to breath. I pull faces from my memory. Katie, Ma, the sisters, Onóra. It is the women that you go on living for. It is the women most hurt when you disappear or die.

Five, four, three, two, I countdown to myself, "go," springing to my feet, racing left close as possible by the house fronts, then, crouched low, I cross to the home alley, moving as fast as I possibly can, I have never raced down the left wing on the pitch any faster, and I hop the wall because the gate makes noise and with quickness that only comes from years of practice slide open the kitchen window and land on the scarred lino floor.

And then I will make no more noise this night. And then I will not move until the sun breaks across the lough. I curl up on the floor of the tiny hall. My back pressed against the base of the stair. And I begin to dream.

30 January 1972

"Time tends to impose order on the past. We look back on the early days and think we discern the outline of what comes later.

"Knowing now how things happened, we assume this is the way it was bound to be.

"But the trajectory wasn't pre-set. The chaos we felt around us was for real, and rich in possibilities other than those which came to pass.

"The well-composed, neatly cropped photograph doesn't always tell the truth. The out-of-focus picture is sometimes more accurate."

- *Eamon McCann in the introduction to* No Go, A Photographic Record of Free Derry, *by Barney McMonagle*

We can lay the blame in so many ways, of course. We can blame so many people, and we do, and yes, they are guilty, yet…

Edward Heath was a monster. A Saddam Hussein of the British Isles. He and Margaret Thatcher have more innocent blood on their hands than any English rulers since Cromwell, and that's quite an accomplishment. General Robert Ford should have been locked up for life in Spandau like the Nazi war criminal he most closely resembled. Major General Andrew MacLennan should have gone to prison as well, a cowardly murderer who did his superior's bidding in the worst traditions of the military. The entire British Conservative Party, which had moved the situation from terrible to disastrous with their ascendance to power, should be held at least as accountable as any Iraqi Baathist. Surely the tyrannical Protestant Unionists at Stormont remain the most guilty of all, still…

The day was a bit cold. Rain was threatening. The sky was winter grey, clouds tumbling over themselves as they rushed in from the sea and fell over the mountains of Donegal. People woke up. Ate breakfast. Went to Mass. I had come home from the night before just in time for angry looks from my Ma and a bowl of her porridge, the thick warmth of which began to cut into the alcohol poisoning. We hadn'a been out. You couldn'a be out. We'd just been holed up in one of the abandoned houses near the foot of Nailor's Row. We'd snuck there in the twilight, close enough to the Brit Fort, as Thomas said, that you could "hear 'em cough." But somehow in our minds – not so close that they could hear us.

I remember seeing Ivan Cooper that morning. He was rushing along the street with three of his mates following. He said, "How'd ya be laddie? You're not giving that Ma of yours too much trouble." "No sir," I told him. "Coming to the march then?" "I'll be with ya," I said. "Good," he smiled, he had stopped and now looked up toward the walls. The march was supposed to go around these symbols and end at the Guildhall, which stood as the emblem of Protestant power. "No trouble from you and your mates though, this is a peaceful Sunday." "No trouble," I answered, "No, sir."

"You claim to be majority / Well you know that its a lie / You're really a minority / On this sweet emerald isle / When Stormont bans our marches / They've got a lot to learn / Internment is no answer / Its those mothers turn to burn!"

The march began as an incredible thing. It looked as if the entire Catholic community had come, and many more. You could not see the end as the line poured down the hill from Creggan, a tidal wave of passion. For the real right to vote. For the real right to jobs. For an end to internment most of all. Let our fathers and brothers and uncles come home from Long Kesh and your secret prisons. Stop arresting people for being Catholic. Stop torturing our men. I remember the mothers especially. The mothers who filled the route because they wanted their men home, and their boys home, and they wanted to stop living in fear.

And Mr. Cooper, well, there he was, speaking from the truck with his megaphone, jumping down to converse and decide, jumping back up to speak again. You know, he was a Protestant himself. He was proof, as of course Parnell and Casement and many others had been, that the religion itself did not automatically destroy one's soul.

Still...

We drifted toward the side as the crowd filled the Bogside streets. Mr. Cooper said we'd be stopping at The Corner, going all the way to the Guildhall might "provoke the violence." And so we could not even march in our own city. The fuckin' Prods could march here anytime they wanted, with the full police escort, and could chant "Kill the Pope, Kill the Taigs," but we could not even go...

"You Anglo pigs and Scotties / Sent to colonise the north / You wave your bloody Union Jack / And you know what its worth! / How dare you hold to ransom / A people proud and free / Keep Ireland for the Irish / Put the English back to sea!"

And there the Paras were. Laughing from William Street, pointing. You could read their lips. They were taunting us. Smacking their rifle butts with their hands. "C'mon you fuckin' potato eating Pope boys, C'mon. Come over here and we'll have a bit of fun."

Yet...

What pulled us there? What drew us to the piles of stones that formed the base of the barricades? The sound truck, the attention, was that way, and we went the other. Did I follow? I followed. Yes. I was not first, or even second or third, or fourth or fifth. I followed. And then the stones were flying, and we were all throwing them. Father Daly yelled at us to stop. I think he did. I think I remember his voice calling to us, "Laddies - don'na give them what they want." Do I really remember hearing that? Did he really say that? Or is it just important for me to know that at that moment we all had choices.

At that moment, we all had choices. We did. They did. We're humans right? We're fucking humans. We're not robots directed by God or military commanders or anyone or anything. We're fucking humans with decisions to make.

"Well, its always Bloody Sunday / In the concentration camps / Keep Falls Road free forever / From the bloody English hands / Repatriate to Britain / All of you who call it home / Leave Ireland to the Irish / Not for London or for Rome!"

And then Jackie was dead on the street, and then Hugh who was not even near us. And then Mr. Doherty who was just trying to run for safety, and then old Bernie McGuigan, who was trying to help Mr. Doherty. And then John just fell off the barricade with a huge hole in his head. And then it was madness, and half the dead were from my class at school. Yes.

Thirteen dead. Another thirteen wounded. And the mothers screamed in agony. They screamed in the streets, and they screamed in hospital, and they screamed in their bedrooms for many nights. And the coffins were lined up in the church. And everyone might have learned. It is a human decision to learn, isn't it? We all might have learned.

We are fucking humans, are we not? We are responsible, we make choices, we are not robots. Is that not true? We can think independently and choose to do this or that, choose to learn this or that, choose to hear this or that.

We are. And now I am old, but my dreams are still filled with those choices. They always will be.

peace

There was this day of summer rain falling over us as we chased each other in the graveyard on the hill. We had pulled our shirts off and kicked our shoes and socks under a thick tree and simply let the water baptise us in the pure joy of childhood.

We were as wet as if we had gone for a swim but raced and hid and tagged and sang, "Oh brave King Brian, he knew the way - To keep the peace and to make the hay: - For those who were bad he cut off their head; - And those who were worse he killed them dead."

We fell on the grass and rolled over graves ancient and recent and laughed, and then the cloudbank broke apart, and the sun exploded through, flashing off our slick skins, and setting a rainbow that crossed the valley.

And then we lay there quietly, in the gentlest of breezes, and closed our eyes.

summer vacation

The sky is a brilliant red over the western edge of the world, and the hills of the Sperrin Highlands have turned the deepest green. Alongside our camp a tiny stream babbles poetry at us as it heads down toward the Mourne in the valley far below.

I have travelled long and hard to get here. With my American university done for the year I packed most of what I actually owned into a backpack, hitch-hiked from East Lansing, Michigan to New York in a brutal fifty-hour experience, slept on the couch of cousins for five days, catching up, and then took the number 6 train to the 7 to the A and then the bus to Kennedy Airport, where I climbed aboard the Aer Lingus 747, fell into the deepest sleep, and awoke in Dublin.

From Dublin I got a ride with a lorry up to Ballybofey, and from there I walked, following the River Finn all the way to Strabane, and then north, walking among the tiny hedge-rimmed fields that defined the extent of Irish poverty, alongside the Foyle to Derry.

I should not have come, of course. I should have stayed on campus and swum in the pool every day prepping for the next season. I should have bartended at Emil's at night making money. I surely should not have crossed the sea to a place where I was on far too many lists, but sometimes the call is just too powerful to resist.

The campfire is burning, and the smell of rashers and eggs is spreading across the grass and clover to where Aedan and I sit, and we smile. This is a beautiful place, a magnificent evening at the end of a perfectly lovely July day, and we have been up and out in this Atlantic air since dawn, and are desperately hungry.

Around us our end of the day work lies on blankets. Small rectangular boxes strapped to sloppily wrapped packages. Explosives surrounding bags of roofing nails. It takes us about fifteen or twenty minutes to assemble each, perhaps, we have no watches and little sense of the hours. And this is boring, boring work, made possible only by the evening breeze, and the company, and the smell of food coming, and the chattering of the magpies that flitter above the gorse.

These nail bombs will liberate us, will they not? They will free us from the Paras and the Constabulary. They will push the Apprentice Boys and the

Orange Order away from us for good. They will smash open the gates of Long Kesh and let the prisoners come home. They will chase the Brits back onto their ships and back to merry ol' England, so that we can live in peace, in our own nation.

And we are fighting the Lord's fight here, are we not? We are the reborn Fenians. The descendents of the ancient giants who built the golden age of Celtic culture a millennium ago. We are the current holders of the torch that has passed from Wolfe Tone to the Young Irishmen to the Brotherhood to Padraic Pearse and the heroes of the 1916 Rising to Michael Collins and the IRA that took 26 counties. And now we must finish the job.

And we are avengers as well, as we must be. For Jackie and Michael and Hugh and Kevin. For Johnny and Gerry and James. All our friends, all our age, all slaughtered in one day, and a dozen more since. Sean, and Michael, and Patrick. Ciallian and Damon and Peter. And maybe most for old Bernie McGuigan, shot dead while waving the white flag for Christssakes. And Tommy Friel and Bobby McGuinness and Joe Walker, all picked off by the rifles of Paras on the streets of our city, in our country.

Niall yells that the food is ready for eating, and we scramble over to join the others. We talk of football and girls left behind. I tell a story or two from the States. Daniel says a few of us will be going to Belfast as the week ends, there is work there to be done.

Later, in the dark, a million stars will fleck the sky above us. Constellations looking down on God's green earth as they have for all time. In a week or so I will be involved in unimaginable things. Things that will haunt forever, though I will not feel them for years. In three weeks I begin to wonder if any of this can possibly make sense, but I will hide my doubts, burying them under youthful bluster. In a month or a bit more, I will retrace my journey, and drop back into life as an American university jock. People will ask me how my summer was, and I will tell them about the green hills, and the salt air, and the streams running toward the sea, and the stars that shine down upon us, letting us know just how small we really are.

daybreak

In the bare cold light of the first dawn the stairs just east of the Bishopsgate are cold and lightly polished by the damp of the night.

I sit there smoking a Camel. Breathing in the last of the night's air. To my left, beyond the gate, lies the old prison block of the half-millennia British Regime. To my right, across the street, the old green steel walls of the Brit fort stand, with video cameras still bristling, though human heartbeats have mostly disappeared from the scene. Behind me the malls and theaters of the new Derry tumble toward the riverbanks. Over there, straight ahead and down the other side of the hill, the Free Derry Corner and the Bogside slumber.

Martin comes through the gate. He looks awful. He looks ancient. Yet, is he five years older than me? or a bit more? I am unsure. I know him immediately, and he me, though it has been at least a decade. He pauses in the middle of Bishops Street. "Who the fuck let a piece of shite like you back into town?" "Where the fuck would the likes of you be going this time o' the morning?" We laugh. I get up and hug him. I light two cigarettes off mine and hand him one, take a deep drag off the two I momentarily hold, than toss the butt in a high arc toward the green fort. It falls and rolls in a tiny shower of sparks before sizzling out on the wet pavement.

He tells me that he is on his way to work. I ask where. He says he does prep stuff at the restaurant on the third floor of Austin's on the Diamond. I say something about that keeping him out of trouble. He says he's heard that I do "interesting things." I tell him that I've always tried to do that.

In 1972 Martin disappeared from home and joined the new Provos. He came back on occasion, often in camouflage and hood, usually with a rifle in hand. We all heard stories. Some were probably true. Then we knew he spent a decade in prison, but there was never really a charge or a trial, so, maybe yes and maybe no. When we told stories about him we made him part of everything. Why not? Did he pull off a bombing in London? in Liverpool? "Hometown boy makes good" kind of thing. Anyway, he came back more than a decade ago. And never said a thing. But we know where he was when Omagh happened, and he didn't do that, and we have all, more or less, decided that if it's from before the Good Friday Agreement, it belongs in the past. This seems either fair or necessary.

"They're gone," he says, pointing to the fort. "That's what the news says this morning. They're done policing." "Still here though," I say. "Ya," he answers, "The wankers are still here, don't know how we'll ever really get rid of 'em." "Not for lack of trying." "Not for lack of trying," he repeats, and it is indescribably sad to hear him say these words. "They'll become irrelevant," I say, "We'll just be Europeans, we'll get the Euro, the evidence of them will disappear."

He finishes the cigarette, asks for another without words. I light two more, pass him one. In synchronized movement we both flick our butts toward the fort. "You were raised to be an optimist," he tells me. "It's those American genetics." Now just I laugh. "'Tis better now? Is it not?" He manages a small smile. "Wouldn'a be better except for the struggle." He stares at me. "Best be on my way," he says, "the coffee will not grind itself." "I'll see you around," I say as he starts down the street. "Go home and go to sleep," he yells back, "I can see you've been up all the night thinking. That's always been bad for ya." "Or I can come by for coffee," I suggest. "We donn'a open til ten, go to sleep til..."

I sit back down. The sunrise is peeling the shadows from the scene. But the stones are still chilled.

She's the belle...

"I'll tell me Ma when I get home, The boys won't leave the girls alone, They pull my hair, they steal my comb, But that's all right till I get home..."

There are names that I do not mention to my Ma. I do not say "Michael" and I do not say "Sean." If I do she cries for her lost children, and I do not have the power to help her heal. So when we talk of the past it is an edited version, of course. And if I tell stories I reconstruct them carefully, filling up seats that now must be left empty with scenery, or reframing the picture so that certain figures now stand outside the frame.

"She is handsome, she is pretty, She's the belle of Belfast city, She's a courting one, two, three, Hey, won't you tell me, who is she?"

My father had a favourite holiday – Halloween. He brought American-style celebrations to our street, he even found gourds, if not pumpkins, to carve, and no one carved more elaborate, complicated, or scary lanterns than he could, though he never demonstrated another artistic inkling. Wild, arched-backed cats screamed from the eyes of his monsters, and the mouths leered like drooling demons. He died on Halloween thirteen years ago now. My Ma lights a candle in a tiny ceramic pumpkin in his memory each October 31st.

"Albert Mooney says he loves her, All the boys are fighting for her, Knock at the door and ring the bell, Hey, my true love, are you well..."

My Da's favourite song was "I'll Tell Me Ma," which he'd sing loudly every Sunday morning, and many others, inserting his name in the appropriate slot. He had met my Ma in Belfast, at the American-run hospital at Musgrave Park out on the Lisburn Road where she was a very young nursing assistant. He had courted her on convalescent walks through that city on the Lagan. First in the leafy south suburbs, then in the darker city centre. Then, along the river opposite the shipyards. And later, around Derry after they had both transferred to the hospital at Ebrington Barracks, and he had come and met the family.

"Out she comes as white as snow, Rings on her fingers, bells on her toes, Our Jenny Murry says she'll die, If she doesn't get the fellow with the roving eye."

He would begin singing as he shaved, and keep going as he came down the stairs. If it was a particularly good morning he would pull me along playing the pipe. If it was a great day and the sun was lighting the hills surrounding us he would get Michael to play the fiddle and Sean to bang on the bodhran, and he would reach the kitchen and swoop Ma away from the stove and into his arms and they would dance through the front room, and once in a great while, right out the door and into the street.

"I'll tell me Ma when I get home, The boys won't leave the girls alone, They pull my hair, they steal my comb, But that's all right till I get home. She is handsome, she is pretty, She's the belle of Belfast city, She's a courting one, two, three, Hey, won't you tell me, who is she?"

But when I remember that in the conversations with my Ma it is just Da singing, and me playing my wee flute, and she laughing, and the neighbors smiling. And those other memories, the boys lost to strange and sad wars, are left tucked softly beneath the green grass of Ireland and America, where they might leave this beautiful woman in peace, as much as might be possible.

"Let the wind and the rain and the hail go high, Snow come tumbling from the sky, She's as nice as apple pie, She'll get a fellow by and by. When she gets a lad of her own, She won't tell her Ma when she gets home, Let them all come as they will, It's Albert Mooney she loves still"

saviour

The priest would come to the house. Yes, this is how it went in that time and place. Parents were not summoned to school, the school came and knocked on your front door and sat and had tea in the front room while, depending on the nature of the failing or the crime or the sin, you either cowered up in your room or stood silently in the corner watching the proceedings.

No one argued with the priest or the brothers in these matters. Not you. Not your parents. This had, I now understand, far less to do with their religious position than with their profession. Honestly, the adults I knew argued with priests anywhere about everything – "Nah father, I can'na believe that would be true," was a common conversation in pubs and on the street – but you could not argue with a teacher. That was the highest calling there was. After all, just a hundred-fifty years before Catholics had hidden in caves to go to school in defiance of English laws against educating the natives. Education mattered more than anything else. And failing in that, or fighting with it, was the greatest of violations.

But I was one of those lads. Couldn't or wouldn't read. They were not sure which. I knew, but I wouldn't let on. "Couldn't" meant I was stupid and hopeless and I'd spend the whole of my life sitting on the kerb or maybe the quayside, smoking fags and collecting from The Dole and spending those quid at the pub. "Wouldn't" implied something else, something much better. I didn'a admit it, but I knew exactly what I was doing. And to make "wouldn't" look right, I had to do the rest. I had to fight everything.

The man who came from Belfast - who came from the Ministry – he decided that I couldn't. "Minimal Brain Damage" he wrote on his chart. I know this because the priest told me this. Told my parents this. Over tea in the front room while I stood silently in the corner, watching. "But I cannot believe this," the priest said. "He does not look 'brain damaged' in any way to my eyes. He looks angry." I blinked rapidly, trying to hide real fear, but then the priest said something else. "And I think he is angry because he is frustrated. Can we solve this?"

People didn't know all the scientific stuff back then. No one did. But great teachers are great teachers, wherever and whenever.

"The Bishop found some of these phonograph records," he continued. "They are from a library for the blind in Belfast. They are books being read, and perhaps books that might interest the lad. You have a phonograph?" he looked around the room, his eyes finding the box, a rare product of Derry's almost lost manufacturing world, "Ah there it would be, wonderful." He reached into a black case and pulled out two dozen albums with simple black lettering on white sleeves. Peeking from the corner I could see that they also had odd bumped symbols along the top.

The priest finished his tea, got up. Thanked Ma and Da and Aunt Onóra for their time and hospitality. Then he stepped across the room and laid his hand on my shoulder and with just that gesture carried me out of the door with him, and into the street, where rain fell as a soft veil. "You might try to listen to some of these lad, and see what you think. There are a few stories there that you would likely find entertaining." He did not smile. He never really did. He said no more that day. He simply walked away. Two days later, awake before anyone else, I put one of the albums on. "*Lyra Celtica*," it said. "The Anthology of Celtic Poetry. Edited by E.A. Sharp and J. Matthay. First Edition Eighteen Hundred and Ninety Six, Revised Nineteen Hundred and Twenty-Four."

The voice was scratchy, the speaker hissed. I assumed that whoever had written this had read it just for me to hear, or for old blind Seamus who sat by Bishopsgate, selling the papers. The disk turned a few more times. "I am the wind which breathes upon the sea, I am the wave of the ocean, I am the murmur of the billows, I am the ox of the seven combats, I am the vulture upon the rocks, I am a beam of the sun, I am the fairest of plants, I am a wild boar in valout, I am a salmon in the water, I am a lake in the plain, I am a word of science, I am the point of the lance of battle, I am the God who creates in the head the fire. Who is it who throws light into the meeting on the mountain? Who announces the ages of the moon - If not I? Who teaches the place where couches the sun - If not I?"

And the world had begun to open.

I got lost on the way from here to Bushmills

James wanted to meet but I was not in the mood to drive to Belfast and he always whines about making the drive "through your fucking outback" because he's an unrepentant big city snob who thinks Belfast is great and Glasgow is somehow better. Jee-sus: Both cities suck. Dark, filthy, monuments to the worst of the industrial revolution that they are.

So I said, "Not a problem mate, we'll meet halfways," but that only generated thirty-six emails, now carefully preserved in sequence by the magic of Google technology, in which we argued over what "halfways" meant, and in which all logical meeting points were rejected by one or the other til we were at this tiny town on the North Coast known for sheep and whiskey. "Is there a pub there?" "Of course there's a pub there, there'd be pubs anywhere." "Is there wireless there?" "Wireless? Not sure there'd be phones, we might be able to get telegrams out though." He didn'a laugh. He doesn't usually enjoy my jokes.

So I awoke early the next day. Very early. The sun was just considering crossing the eastern horizon. And I had something like breakfast. Coffee and brown bread with local butter and French blueberry preserves. I ate while reading Nick Hornby's *A Long Way Down*, starting it, actually. It had ended up on top of a pile of books after I had accidentally knocked the pile over two weeks before and last night decided to finally, OK, under some pressure, pick them up. When I did, this unread hardcover, bought barely used but heavily discounted from a bookseller in Dalkey six months earlier, found its way to the pinnacle, from which it was picked sometime after I pulled on boxers and a t-shirt as I climbed out of bed. *"Can I explain why I wanted to jump off the top of a tower block? Of course I can explain why I wanted to jump off the top of a tower block. I'm not a bloody idiot. I can explain it because it wasn't inexplicable: it was a logical decision, the product of proper thought. It wasn't even very serious thought, either. I don't mean it was whimsical - I just meant that it wasn't terribly complicated, or agonised. Put it this way: say you were, I don't know, an assistant bank manager, in Guildford. And you'd been thinking of emigrating, and then you were offered the job of managing a bank in Sydney. Well, even though it's a pretty straightforward decision, you'd still have to think for a bit, wouldn't you? You'd at least have to work out whether you could bear to move, whether you could leave your friends and colleagues behind, whether you could uproot your wife and kids. You might sit down with a bit of paper and draw up a list of pros and cons."*

Reading a book about four wanna-be suicides has to be the best way to start a day, right? Right. I admitted to myself, those French preserves still in my mouth, that at many points in my life I might have joined the crowd atop the fifteen-story block on any number of given nights. I've stood higher, more alone, with better plans. But, the losses seem less strangling now. Eventually there are so many tiny wounds that you have confidence either that you will survive or that you will bleed out naturally. Either way, there would be no reason to rush things.

And then I showered and even shaved and pulled on clothing and climbed into the car, tossing my overweight backpack with its multiple laptops and piles of paper, onto the left seat. Punched a radio button that gave me the BBC World Service, and started on my way.

I crossed the Craigovan and took the first real left off the roundabout and headed north along the leeward coast of Lough Foyle. Oh, I suppose there might be other ways. There are, usually, a choice of routes, but I am a conservative in early morning road choices. Familiarity requires less vision. And soon I am running above the Waterside. That other side of the river - where lawns are wide and green and kids grow up riding horses and playing tennis on grass courts. I find it funny now that I can look at these houses and dream of striking it rich – that big hit novel? – and living in a place like this. That was once so unimaginable.

James called my mobile then. I have his ringtone set to Jumpin' Jack Flash. This is a mistake. But one still uncorrected. He was still in bed. "You're on the road?" He was stunned. "I just always assume you'll be late." "I could still be late," I told him, "but get your arse moving." I wished I could get off the road, honestly. I wish I could cut across the fields as I had on escapes as a boy. Roads constrict what you see. Motorways cut that to nothing. You know a landscape when you move through urban alleys or rural fields, when you climb over walls, when you see what is behind what people intend you to see.

I stopped in Coleraine. The sun was breaking through the rain clouds left from the night before. I did take away coffee and sat on a wall near the church across from the Woolworth. "Many New Household Appliances. Big Red Book Summer Savings. My Garden Gazebo £19.99." The wind coming straight down from the north was cold. I opened the book again. The book I had carried with me as a costume – "just a tourist on holiday" – as if my reasons for travelling were any less exotic. The four suicidals had stepped from the roof, off on a mission to help one of the group. Progress. I realised that the best cure for suicidal ideation is always someone else's crisis. At least for me. Creates a self-sense of value and also a "maybe they're worse off than me" kind of superiority. Besides. Unless you are a complete exhibitionist suicide is a solitary thing. Someone else's crisis intruding on you means you are not alone.

From Coleraine I took the even longer Portstewart route. Sticking to the cliff edge as much as the need for pavement under the Micra's tiny wheels might allow. There are good chippers in Portrush, but it was too early for that, so I rolled through, but then...

The next few hours may have included The Giant's Head and Dunluce and White Rocks and a few pints in Portballintrae. Is it five kilometres from Portrush to Bushmills? No, a bit longer. Eight perhaps. maps.google.co.uk suggests thirteen minutes even with the Portballintrae detour. It took me fifteen times that, or twenty.

But sometimes I get lost in time and place and there are memories to visit in each of these spots. Rich ones. Scary ones. Romantic ones. Sharp ones. And every one needed the time required.

"How the fuck did I beat you here," James asked as I stepped into the Gas Bar at the Bushmills Inn. "Ya know," I said. "Yeah," he did. I was hungry. Before we could look at the four computer screens we now spread under the antique gas lighting, before we could begin to compare budget ideas, and web design ideas, and what the "we need your support" letters might look like, I needed a shot or two and a Smithwicks or two and a round of stew. "Local sheep, very good," I pronounced. The barkeep looked troubled.

Afterwards we walked out into the disappearing day, headed to our cars. We could feel the imminent rain. "Lovely little village," James said. "Don'na really know it," I answered, "never could get quite this far east as a kid." "They probably needed to keep the likes of you away from the distilleries." There might have been truth to that.

It was a downpour on the way back to Derry. All the oncoming headlamps arrived first as twisting stars through the filter of the storm. There've been days when I've thought about turning right into an explosive and deadly crash. But not tonight. Not this week. Not this month.

ring

I looked at my mobile as it rang and stared. I had not even recalled transferring that identity over to this new phone, and that was more than a year ago, but then, there it was. Her name.

I paused. It is hard to know what to do. She hurt me really badly. Really. Far more than she should have, but yes, guys are weak, we fall too hard, we believe too much. Yet, it was all in the way past now, and a different woman, a woman truly right for me, fills my life with joy these days, and I had even tried, long ago, to mend this angry split. One late night, staring out a dirty window at a fragment of the Foyle flowing north, I had emailed her: "Just wanted to say hello," I wrote, "Just wanted you to know that today I was in a conversation and I said something and realised that I had learned that from you. And that made me think of the many ways in which you enriched my life. And that made me happy. So I wanted to let you know that it is not all bitterness, and the anger is gone, and I really wish you well."

In the morning I awoke to a two-thousand word rant about how I had been "too dependent."

So, I figured, that would be that.

And months went by, thirty-six of them? Maybe more.

I thought and thought, then opened the phone. "Good morning," I said, as coolly as I might muster. "Did you just drive past my house?" "No." "Really? I was sitting on my porch and was sure I saw your car." "I'm in East Lansing, so, no." "Oh, I thought you might be going to the pool and I was going to say, turn around and come have a smoke and a beer." "Sorry, ninety miles away."

There was a long quiet. "I just was thinking 'bout you, and wanted to let you know that my dad died." "I'm sorry," I said – genuinely – her dad was a wonderful man, even if he thought I was a dangerously lapsed Catholic. I asked how she was, how her mom was. I said the right things, but then, "He died in February, I meant to call you."

Now I understood. It is June. She always wanted a deep relationship from June through Mid-August, and from Thanksgiving through Valentine's Day. The rest of the time she was "too busy," her own mix of calendars academic and romantic. For two years we got together and broke up like clockwork. It made sense to her, it made me insane.

"When you're in town some afternoon, come on over," she said, "You know the summer me, always a good time."

I didn't really want any more conflict. "I'll try and do that," I said. "That would be nice." Which might have been true, except for those memories I just could not shake.

history lesson

We end up hopelessly lost. I should know better than to try to dodge Belfast by wandering west, but I was in no mood for traffic or motorways and so ended up deep in the Englishy countryside between Lisburn and Lough Neagh. But the sun is swimming in a clear blue sky and the roof is open and the CD player is blaring Janis Joplin, so who really cares?

Was this Upper Ballinderry or Lower Ballinderry? No matter. Here the cows fill the fields, unlike the sheep that dominate further north, and the roads wind through the landscape, from James's barn to Rory's front door, from Kieran's Pub to where Michael left his plow, I'm guessing, of course, but it could not have been any other way in the planning, unless massive quantities of alcohol were involved. Maybe some of the former and some of the latter.

At a place called the Horseshoe Inn we ask for a late lunch to go and directions. The food turns out to be much finer than the advice. But we end up eating by an antique lock on the Lagan Navigational Canal in Aghalee, a tiny village that sits in a spectacular glen called Friary. The canal once brought the Lough and the River Bann and the sea together and fueled a mill industry, weaving cotton and wool and further Scoticizing this corner of Ireland. When it closed in the 50s the decline began that has only recently reversed as this has become a Belfast suburb. And then we make one more wrong turn and end up at Moira, or Maigh Rath, where, almost 1,400 years ago a High King of Tara defeated Comgall, the High King of Ulster in epic battle.

"How do you know all this stuff?" she wonders. "I could hardly tell you when Michigan became a state." "Ah," I tell her, "but that's not much of a story, now is it? So why would ya remember? Congress taking a boring vote can'na compare with what we've got here."

"Is it really better history, or are you just all better storytellers?"

"I think we are better listeners," I tell her. "We learn from early on to hear all the stories these ancient places tell, even the ones most deeply buried."

She does not say what I know she is thinking. There's the famous quote, "The problem with Americans is that they do not know history. The problem with Europeans is that they do." And she is wholly American, and though she does love the stories, she sees a world of deadly traps in these memories.

"We've forgiven the southerners, ya know," I explain. "For what?" "For

Maigh Rath, for the invasion that Cuchulainn defeated, even for the Treaty." "How generous," and she laughs.

It is getting quite dark before we've found the motorway and crossed the River Boyne on a very twenty-first century bridge. Despite going 120 I hear thousands of voices calling from this place, from the depths of the history of colonisation. But I don't say anything. We'll just pay the toll and head for a late dinner around Drogheda.

storm

The ferry left from Rosslare amidst fog and a hard rain – and once the turn to starboard beyond the breakwater had been made – much the last of the afternoon colour drained away. Despite that I had climbed to my favourite spot, along the rail just below the optimistically named Sun Deck, and stood, leaning against windscreen windows, smoking a cigarette and trying to keep my feet on the slippery, lurching surface while I stared at a sea that faded, in not more than a hundred meters, into a thickly draped curtain of grey.

This, for me, is not necessarily a bad thing. Sailing in beautiful weather is lovely, yet, crossing this edge of the Atlantic in heavier weather is a healthy reminder that living on islands comes with a certain set of costs.

I had an appointment in France that I did not want to get to. So, instead of the €29 or less, one-and-a-half-hour flight from Dublin to Charles deGaulle Airport I had chosen to drive south for more than two hours into Wexford County and spent €140 for a nineteen hour boat ride to Cherbourg that would still leave me four or more hours from my destination, assuming I maintained speed while driving with the steering wheel suddenly on the wrong side of the car. They told me they'd pay for me to come. As many have learned, they had no real idea of how I might take that.

Up on the north coast of Ulster the sea is wild but the crossing might be short. That "Celtic Crossroads" is less than 60 km no matter how you slice it, Eirann to Alba. But this, which also ties ancient Celtic lands together, is many times that as you wrap around the south-west edge of England and cross what seems very much like open ocean. In the days before the Franks pushed their way to the Atlantic through Normandy this was as much Celtic heartland as any, surely some set out in their tiny craft to share, to trade, to explore. I tossed a last cigarette into the sea, humbled by that thought. They were so brave in the face of the then unknowable, and I was afraid of speaking to the too-well-known who were funding my research.

So I climbed below. It was just half-five and the night was very young. The darkness outside made the usually too bright pub acceptable in atmosphere. I sat down, ordered a pint and a whiskey and pulled a book and two reports from a dripping backpack. The book was my threadbare reminder that even those of us who have lived too long on the borderlines can survive if we learn just enough of the rules. I have read and re-read it more than a dozen times. I have never broken the childhood desire for the repetition of favourite stories. The reports were on project funding and possible research expansions. They were filled with things that didn't quite add up. I knew that. Things that people might be angry about. I knew that too. Things that would make those sitting in Paris doubt my competence, I assumed. I turned and looked out. Rain pelted the glass. Whenever things go wrong I retreat into the character of a scared ten-year-old ready to get whacked by the priest, or a scared seven-year-old with Da coming home when things have occurred, or a scared fourteen-year-old with soldiers searching my possessions. The fear strips away all else.

The whiskey warmed me in a blast and I ordered another. I opened both reports but the print blurred in front of my eyes. Maybe in the morning, I thought, and let them fall closed. I picked up the book, surprised to see something in it acting as a bookmark. I took a long drink from the pint and opened to the suggested page. The marker was an antique postal card of the walls of Derry, looking down onto the Bogside. "The Walls of the Maiden City," it said, "have never been breached." It was copyrighted 1963, "Londonderry, Northern Ireland, United Kingdom," but had never been posted or even addressed. In the lower right corner there was a tiny pink heart and the words, "We believe in each other."

On the page, well, you understand, I have read the book more than a dozen times, so I knew immediately, but I threw down the second whiskey and read, "We met… and from then on, it became impossible ever again to give up completely. I have given some thought to why this should be. I believe it was love. When once you have encountered it, you will never sink again. Then you will always yearn for the light and the surface."

I finished the pint. There are those of us, I thought, who just keep trying. Just keep pulling ourselves up from the floor, no matter how badly the last blow has hurt us. In my best spirits I believe that I am one of those people. So I ordered dinner to go, and coffee with it, and walked to the cabin charged to my benefactors, and lay down on the upper berth. I decided that I would let both this night and the shore of France come to me. I opened the book again, this time to page one. "We ascended toward the light, five floors up, and split up into thirteen rows facing the god who unlocks the gates of morning." "It is all narrative," I remembered a favourite professor saying. And I believe that. I would tell them the story they needed when I arrived in Paris, and I thought that I might be all right. The boat rolled on the waters. I read until almost dawn, and then I slept.

night and fog

I have spent this moonless night sleepless, walking on the Embankment and along the quaysides from the bridge on north until there wasn't much point and then back again. And then I walked backed into the city, past the Guildhall, through the Ferryquay gate, and up the "steepest high street in the United Kingdom" to The Diamond, where, hopelessly exhausted in too many ways, I smoke four cigarettes in succession at the foot of the Great War Memorial. Below me the fog has rolled fully in, filling all below this most ancient hill with the hundreds of thousands of ghosts of nine millennia of history.

I toss the fourth butt onto the damp pavement and watch it dim into oblivion. When those ancient travellers first came to this spot high above the fresh waters they were close enough to the ice age – closer than we are to the Trojan War – that their stories may have told of the glaciers backing up across the European plain. Did they look towards that open sea and pray to the spirits of the earth that spring and summer would stay with them and let their barley grow?

Tonight the air is velvet. Thick but languid, and I descend from the heights of mythic history down into the personal. Following Butcher Street through the walls and descending Fahan Street to the Bogside, it is eighty or a hundred meters down, pausing briefly at St. Columb's Wells, where, in this vapour, the stone city of my youth still might be alive in ways impossible in the light of day. The Free Derry corner is frozen in silence as I move through, tripping and falling by the monuments to Bloody Sunday. But I need not see these in detail now, the names carved here are burned into memory. So many were my age. There is so much anger that I keep working to abandon. OK, yes, enough of that – really. I think I should choose my ghosts with more care, for near this corner also run the spirits of the greatest and closest friends of my life, and the whispered recall of thousands of hours of play.

So, I climb back to my feet and I realise that I should walk back home and curl into bed before sunrise strikes, but then, I certainly know that I rarely do as I should. Instead I begin to climb again, up the Creggan Road, out of this old neighborhood, and slowly, as I pass the school, out of the fog bank. This, my grandfather taught me, is where the magic of the Donegal Hills begins. The lands the Tuatha Dé Danann called home. The hills and glens where the Fenians still wait for the moment of redemption. And I keep going. As dawn breaks over the north coast I find myself on the Buncrana

Road past Benview, at the now unmarked and barely noticed border, and here I turn around. I leave behind me the memories of checkpoints and soldiers, and look toward the greens and golds that flash through the sky as the sun cuts through the far horizon illuminating the clouds that still hang beneath where I stand.

I light another cigarette and spend seven minutes watching the world wake. And then I start back down, hungry and ready for breakfast.

Los San Patricios

It was important to the three old men who sat outside the pub on William Street that we know that some of Los San Patricios were from Derry. Perhaps in a place of lost causes we needed to recall them all. For it is not just the winners in history who must be remembered.

All those who made the right decisions but whom did not receive the right rewards. Who better to celebrate? The winners already got theirs. Those who sought evil, well, they'll get theirs. Those who never tried have already died the death of anonymity.

So each August the three old men would spend a week telling the saga of those who knew wrong and colonialism when they saw it, and who gave up the last of what they had to fight on the side of the angels. And we would sit at their feet, very literally, and absorb the tale, which always began, "In Connemara, in the town of Clifden, a Mexican flag still flies every day, because the oppressed must know that they must stay together…"

And the story would flow. How these first Irish immigrants, fleeing the famine, found themselves instant recruits to a US Army heading to war. Many went almost directly from one ship docking at the Hudson River piers to another ship carrying the raw troops to Texas. That many of these men quickly discovered that their new nation was just one more Protestant power invading and seizing the land of Catholic peasants. And how they made the decision to change sides, and fight for those protecting their homeland.

Like all sagas this one had a songlike quality to it, peaking at the moment on the 20th of August in Eighteen-Hundred and Forty-Seven at the Battle of Churubusco, a moment of unmatched heroism and defiance of the odds, as these brave Irish warriors fought against an unbeatable tide. Like all great oral tradition tales, the family names of Derry would appear, as the ramparts of the convent so far away were defended. And then the chorus, the oppresssed helping the oppressed, would recycle, and then would come the saddest verse, the mass hangings by US Generals.

Yet that song would not end in desolation. It came back to Mexicans celebrating their Irish volunteers and those in the hometown of leader John Riley celebrating their support for Mexico, and finally, to our being instructted to remember to do what was right, even if the cost seemed far too high.

And that week, when we played war in the streets, instead of it being

Fenians against the Brits, it was Los San Patricios – oh so badly pronounced – against the Americans, as we still tried to use fantasy to reverse the degradations of history.

The Morning After

"Huh," I say, pointing to something pink that lies along the tracks. "That wouldn'a be yours, would it?" She kicks me in the shin, which hurts a lot. "The shite you get me into," she says, "I was a pretty nice girl before I met you." "Well, we should never be drinking alcohol from a can," I declare, "It leads to trouble."

We'd walked back to the DART at Grand Canal Dock from where we'd crashed at Aedan's and climbed the stairs and bought the ticket to Dalkey and pushed through the turnstiles and walked to the far end of the platform where I'd lit my cigarette. Below the Canal widens from its narrow path to what must have once been a Dickensian dockyard, the ancient brick and stone buildings surrounding it drop straight into the water, with their freight doors awaiting the teas from China and cottons from the New World and silks and spices from India, as well as, as I'd suggested at some point last night when we'd been right here, the thieves, rogues, and scoundrels who would have patrolled such precincts in the days of whale oil lamps casting only tiny yellow flickering moments in a vast fog-bound darkness.

On the way here in this hazy morning sun I had poured Lucozade from the Spar into me and unsuccessfully attempted to get her to do the same, I am a believer in rehydration as the hangover cure, and was now hoping that a massive nicotine injection would finish the task.

"You should climb down and pick that up." "I didn't drop it." "But you got it off, and that started the whole thing." "Yeah," I said smiling, and she kicked me again. It is sometimes amazing how maturity drops away when drowned in the pints of a half dozen pubs and a four pack of Guinness for the road. Amazing, and, ya know, a great thing, it is important to have those moments when you can't possibly keep your hands off of each other.

"I spent dearly on that bra," she complains. "I'll buy you a new one." "Damn right you will." "Monday, when we're back in the city." "That and more," she finishes.

But then she smiles, just a touch, and leans on my shoulder. "You're still the craziest boy from the north that they allow into Dublin." And I toss the cigarette butt out onto the evidence below and say, "And you're the most beautiful girl they let escape from the States." And then the train roars in and we walk on and fall asleep hanging onto each other.

for Owen who did not think Donegal had proper beaches

I say it again, "this is pretty much the end of the earth," and she just smiles. "Well, certainly," I admit, "there are the Faroes out lost in the fog somewhere beyond and even past that Iceland sure, but that's really only for Vikings and drunk Germans who like to get naked in the hot pools," and she just laughs." But really it is just wild water until it turns to ice and ice until you're going south again and the ice turns into Siberia."

"I like your geography," she whispers.

The fire has grown so big on the diet of driftwood and grasses that we have backed away a bit and now the frame includes the morning light on the Atlantic, and grey-white sands, and far, far, off, the curve of the planet. Earth's true sounds surround us, the surf, the wind rustling the turf behind us, the momentary yelps of the sea birds. She lies on the Hudson's Bay blanket, a trophy of my childhood, with her head resting in my lap, and I watch her breath, slowly, it is incredibly intimate.

When I need peace, I think to myself, I have always come to where the sea meets the land. Because it is at this most primal borderline that we can see in the most directions. Not just up to the heavens and down into the briny deep, not just endlessly north or west or east or south, but forward and backward along the timeline of creation.

She has fallen asleep. Her breath softening to almost silent. I stretch my legs out and dig my toes into the sand. The surface is sun-baked and fragile. Beneath, it grows harder and damper and colder.

From the east the sun continues to arc into the high blue and I know it will be a spectacular day. We will eat something when she awakes again. And then we will run into the ocean and play until we freeze. And then we will warm each other as the tide chants its poetry.

one

I had found a shared third floor brownstone apartment in Fort Greene, just up a long grey hill from Brooklyn's downtown. The three-room flat was shared with the ex-girlfriend of an old friend. We knew each other intimately though not in any way sexually. The front door and kitchen were in my bedroom, the bathroom in hers, so privacy did not exist, but she dressed entirely in black and pretended to be deep, deep into the CBGB's culture, but failed to successfully pull this dark costume over her sunny suburban Florida personality structure. The failed pose kept me away from her no matter how often I would get erections in the night.

But living on South Oxford Street had its rewards. Inner Brooklyn and Lower Manhattan became mine. Dusk might find me getting high in the middle of the Brooklyn Bridge, or hanging on the Trade Center Plaza, or sitting on the Promenade in the Heights as the sunset coloured the harbour, or just drinking a beer at the top of Fort Greene Park with my back resting on the enormous Prison Ships Martyrs Monument – eleven thousand murdered Revolutionary War American prisoners buried in the vault beneath me. This tribute to one more brutal British colonial crime made me feel at home.

And the landlords, a gay couple, CBS producers both, cast me in plays at the Brooklyn Heights Playhouse, letting the actor in me thrive, teaching me to slip into the lives of others. So I twisted myself into *The Elephant Man* and got naked for *Equus* and faked the full American accent for *True West*, and after performances went to the most outrageous parties in the world and did more things than I can recount, but also, sure, turned down more possibilities than I could have ever imagined just a year or two before.

I dabbled in architecture courses at Pratt Institute, and went to work there as a day job. I learned everything about Brooklyn and New York, past and present, and led visitors and new students on elaborate tours while I designed strange buildings more at home in the 19th than 20th Century and developed a reputation for being interesting but difficult.

I also met cops there at Pratt. The old 88th Precinct stood right next to the campus, and, working in admissions, I was supposed to stay in touch – safety being a major issue in recruitment to a college located on the edge of

Bedford-Stuyvesant just a few years after the 1977 blackout riots. And for the first time in my life, I found myself liking cops.

For two years I drifted, just thrilled to be in this city. Playing football in the lobby of One World Trade Center or having sex on the vast "beach" just west of there where one day the World Financial Center would rise. Riding subways to every possible adventure. Dancing in the wildest bars and at private parties in abandoned lofts. Drawing imaginary buildings and swimming in the Atlantic at Coney Island. Skating right at the edge of the insanity of New York City as Reagan and Koch ushered in an era where everyone was poor, sure, but then, no one cared what you did either.

Then a cop named Costello, a classic New York patrolman who twirled his nightstick better than any cheerleader could hope to, and who pronounced his name correctly – the Irish way, grabbed me in the New Alibi Club one late Saturday night. "Lad, you need a real life, and they're about to give the police test. You should cut out all this shite and join us." And having little else on my agenda for the summer, I decided to do that.

two

I was on the muster deck for one of the last times. Graduation was just days away, and everything was fine now. I had dodged the danger of finishing first in my class by throwing the final exam, answering two "integrity" questions wrong deliberately, so they wouldn't have to deal with a trouble-making dyslexic foreigner making a speech in Madison Square Garden. I already knew that I'd be assigned back to the Gun Interdiction Unit where I'd already spent two four week periods playing undercover. I knew that very soon I'd no longer have to worry about shining shoes and ironing uniform shirts.

But the morning was already hot. It was June and the humidity was weighting the air, and I stood at attention sweating in the summer blouse, the clip of the damn clip-on tie rubbing against my throat. God knows I hated every minute of this six months. The interminable class sessions, law, law, law, and more law. The boredom of police procedures. The struggles with the psychologies of this nation that I only half knew. The misery of running five miles each day in a gym whose circumference measured just a twelfth of a mile - that's 60 laps, or as I'd say, 240 corners coming at you. The horror of too many rules suddenly imposed on an unruly life. An instructor was doing inspection and was now yelling at me. He screamed that it looked like I had, "Shined my shoes with a brick." I just smiled, and yelled back, "Sir, a brick was the only thing I could find this morning, Sir. So at least I tried, Sir!" A wave of laughter rolled around the 900 cadets on the deck. The instructor was black but now turned visibly red. But it was too late. It was the final days. So he spun into a perfect right-face and moved on.

Now, seeking stability, I was sharing a house out on the northern edge of Midwood. "Mythical Midwood" I called it. It looked so much like how I imagined an old Ohio town might appear. There was the little main street anchored by the Midwood Theater, the spire of the main hall of Brooklyn College, the huge American football stadium for Midwood High, the little grocery stores and post office – the neighborhood did not seem "New York City" at all. And neither did the house, a 17-room Victorian on a tiny street that dead ended into the cut for the Brighton Line.

The Brighton Line was the D-train back then. And the M, and sometimes the QB, but mostly the D, and when you went to the subway stations you were offered the magical choice of directions: "Trains to New York" one platform said, "Trains to Coney Island" the other offered. In the morning there would be crowds of students for the college and the Murrow High School for broadcasting. On weekend nights beach chairs and Latin music would fill the cars along with the scent of baby oil and Coppertone and Miller High Life. On weeknights it could get lonely and scary, the subways of that moment being a graffiti covered mess.

Kevin and Annie, from Stranolar on the Finn way back when, and Margie, who was somehow from Atlanta and had stumbled into the mix after meeting Kevin at the School of Visual Arts, lived in this grand place for four hundred American bucks a month plus all that we could spend on heating a house that was three stories high and had fourteen foot ceilings downstairs. I had an octagon bedroom that opened onto a second-floor sun porch. Kevin and Annie shared the third floor, bedroom, bath, and mammoth strange space that was probably once a nursery and which connected to an attic where Kevin shot vaguely disturbing nudes. Margie had a big second floor room and used one of the bathtubs and an enormous closet for processsing colour photography. We had big parties for our Manhattan and downtown Brooklyn friends, offering escapes from their space-challenged lives. At those parties we'd turn the bidet on high, it came very close to the ceiling, and aimed coloured lights at it, to give the bathroom atmosphere.

Annie taught in some rich kid private school in the Heights, a "Kennedy kid" kind of place. Kevin and Maggie were artists. I struggled with the Academy, and ran the streets in off hours to get away from the Supreme

Court decisions and other stresses, jogging south on East Seventeenth Street, then west on Avenue H – ducking under the subway tracks by the ancient front-porched wooden station, then south again across the old LIRR dock line, then east on Avenue J, the main street, past the Kosher stores catering to immigrant Israelis and the Halal shops catering to immigrant Palestinians, then, with an ocean breeze in my face toward the Atlantic on the broad width of Ocean Parkway. I might turn around at Kings Highway, or at Avenue X just because "Avenue X" was such a cool name," or if frustration had built to a maximum and it was warm enough I'd go all the way to the sea at Brighton Beach and kick off my shoes and run into the waves.

If more mentally but less physically needy, I'd head north to Prospect Park and wander the Long Meadow or sit by the lake or cross the street and while away hours in the Library, or among the wonders of the Museum, or, in the right weather, fall into fantasies on the Cherry Lawn or in the Japanese Garden of the Brooklyn Botanic Garden. I remember one Saturday afternoon spent simply sitting on the Library steps, below those mammoth gold literary allusions, watching the traffic flow around the Grand Army Arch and the clouds scuttle above the sculpture of winged victory in her chariot. There was much peace in that.

And five days a week I rode the train to Manhattan's 23rd Street, and went to nine hours of classes, and learned all the law and all the procedure and all the self-defense and combat skills, and gave too many smart-mouthed answers, as they say, and fought the rules too often, but did too well for them to seriously mess with me. Plus, I'd already been sucked into undercover work, due to that entertaining accent and a perceived "ethical flexibility." I had made myself valuable.

Now it was late June, and there was this target picked out for me, maybe Provos, probably the INLA, and graduation was coming on Saturday. I floated through this hot day. Got hassled by my law professor for my intentionally wrong answers – "a motorist offers you and your partner $50 to not give him a summons, the correct procedure is…" "C. Put it in your pocket, give half to your partner later, but give the summons anyway." – and defended myself with a series of shrugs.

At half four in the afternoon, or was this 1630 hours, I rode the D train home, the air conditioning not working in the sealed car. We do not have this kind of heat where I am from but I had surely learned it in university in the North American Midwest. The heat and the exhaustion of the day made me sleepy, and I floated in and out of consciousness, and in and out of worlds. When my eyes opened I was thundering through Brooklyn, when they closed I was staring at an angry grey sea on the Irish north coast. When my eyes opened I was this agent of responsibility in the world's greatest city. When they closed I was only myself finding the storms of nature preferable to the storms of humanity. I flickered in this twilight zone for a bit too long.

When I fully woke up the train was screeching through the curve into Brighton Beach, way past my stop at Newkirk Avenue. I got off anyway, and went down onto the street. I bought a Coke and two potato knishes from Mrs. Stahl's at the corner. They were hot and fresh, and smothered with rough mustard, absolutely delicious. I ate them walking to the beach, and then, pulling off just shoes and socks, walked into the water. I had just two days of the Academy left, and two more pair of cadet pants, and did not care at all.

three

The New York City Police Department Firearms Transport Interdiction Unit, called "GIU," hid in the upper level of the 88th Precinct Station House, with access to the ancient fire tower through a ladder in a closet and the most remarkable views of Manhattan's skyline, which appeared to bend around us from our vantage point looking north at the East River.

Actually, all that was there were walls the green of the old police cars from the 1960s, plenty of ash trays, two offices, a table with eight chairs and three stools, and a bunch of lockers with plywood boxes stacked on top where the bosses would dump the files that were our constant homework. Photographs and dossiers, intelligence reports and profiles, crime reports and Interpol briefings that all had to be digested if we were to have any chance at accomplishing anything.

At the end of the academy graduation I took three weeks off. No one else did that, but I had already worked 80 hours of overtime, translating into 120 hours of vacation time, translating into, hmmm, well, math is not my strong point, but around 14 days, plus, six months in the academy had already built up nine "chart days" to take, and there was a week and a half accrued vacation time already, so, they let me go.

I partied for a couple of days with New York friends who were deeply dismayed by my new career. The general terms were "traitor" and "Storm Trooper," and what can you really say? And then I flew "home" via Dublin, where this change in employment was met with a different brand of trouble.

Everyone in the north of Ireland has a relative that is or was a New York, Boston, or Chicago cop, there is nothing seen as wrong in that. No one would have joined the police force in the north, certainly, but they wouldn'a been allowed either, so... but New York at this moment was viewed as only slightly less dangerous than the homeland itself. "Are ye sure lad," I was asked over and over, "They've been shooting the police in New York these days, it's on the news all the time." I promised that I'd stay safe. I promised that I'd wear the bulletproof vest that Yoko Ono gave each new cop in the city. I promised I'd do nothing stupid. All of which were lies, but these are the things you say.

Before I left to return, I had my big moment. Harassed by a soldier I pulled the shield and ID Card from my pocket as identification. The big guy in the green combat uniform turned even whiter than usual, backed away, waved me on. They surely wanted no trouble with Americans, especially an American whose story might end up in a New York newspaper.

Back in Brooklyn I made up a story even for friends and family. I was working, I told them, on an intelligence thing, flying a desk in plainclothes, using my knowledge of Europe to help break up an Italian heroin-smuggling ring. It made little sense, but it was not that cover which was critical.

You are now Patrick McDonough. You are from Newry originally, came to New York in 1976 with a student visa for Brooklyn College, dropped out and stayed. You've been working at The World on Second at Avenue C for the past two years... yeah it's covered. "Uch," I responded, "The World? That place is creepy." *Yeah, they said, we know you know. Your face was familiar when we set this up. They handed me a list of the recently dead in northern Ireland. Who might you know that might create motive? Pick a name, we'll get you enough backstory.*

In the big house in Midwood I pretended I was getting deeply involved. The friends were used to not seeing the women in my life, so it worked. It explained the long disappearances and the erratic behaviors. Out on the streets I began to work toward contacts. Conversations designed to be overheard in the right places. Carefully chosen hang outs. Public fits of anger and violence targeting the right audience, culminating in a carefully staged fight with uniformed cops on West 41st Street that left me with an unplanned concussion.

These guns are all coming from Miami or Virginia and heading to Kennedy Airport. But the pay off is that maybe half are getting diverted to Dominican drug gangs here. "Dominican drug gangs?" I asked. *Yeah, they might be readying for a war with the Jamaicans.* "Whatever," I said, "I'm confused." *It doesn't matter to you, we just need names and transfer places and wiretap targets.* "Sure," I told them. "Why not?"

Two weeks after my "fight" I got invited to move in with the targets. And I did. And my world grew endlessly confusing. Summer in New York is typically brutally hot, especially among the un-air-conditioned, and the fatigue bought by the heat and the fear that prevented any kind of deep sleep, and the days at a time away from home, and away from the cops who were supposedly "my partners," left me completely unsure of who I was each time I opened my eyes.

You're doing good work, kid, I was told over and over again in hurried conversations in the strangest places around New York City. You're doing good work. Might want to stop in at a hospital and check that wound on your arm, looks infected? Go to St. Vincent's, we'll have them look for you. And hey, see what you can dig up on a guy called "Dongo" in Union City in Jersey. "How the fuck am I gonna do that?" *Just ask around kid, you know, just ask and listen, you're doing good work. Are those needle marks on your arm? Be careful kid.*

When I did fall asleep my dreams pulled me back to the streets of Derry. What I had escaped from was now becoming the escape from where I was. Life kicks you in the balls that way. And the dreams got so real that I was sure I was speaking out loud and would give myself away. So I stopped sleeping all together. And July turned to August and August sweltered, and none of the wounds on my body were healing.

four

Life undercover is not like it is on television. Actually, no part of being a cop is like it is on television. People used to ask, "Is it like *Hill Street Blues?*" and I would say, "No, more like *Barney Miller*," which was generally true, but not for me. Actually, a film had appeared a year before that showed a momentary glimpse – *Prince of the City* had this scene where the hero chases down a drug user to steal heroin for another drug user in a series of filthy abandoned buildings in East New York. Laws don't mean a whole lot when you are enforcing the law.

And I had no real police experience yet, so my attempt to be on that "side of the good" had just turned me into a criminal snitch with good benefits and accrued vacation time. It made so little sense in any way, and I couldn't ask anyone, and I couldn't tell anyone. The world was getting so very small so very quickly.

The doctor is cutting something out of the wound in my forearm, glass shards dug deep in amidst green shit that looks really bad. You being sure to use clean needles? "Huh?" I say. *Listen, I don't care who you work for or what they have you doing, but I can probably fix the addiction better than I can fix hepatitis that's run too long.* "Not a problem," I tell him. *Bullshit, he says. Who the fuck do you think you're kidding? The nurse comes in, I drop my shorts and she jabs my ass with penicillin. No follow up, the doctor says, I probably won't see you again until after you're dead. After he's finished, a new bandage wrapped around the wound, the brown stains of antiseptics spilled across the back of my hand, they send me out a back way, and I walk a long thin alley filled with medical waste trash bags, until I reach the lower end of Seventh Avenue.*

One night I break into a liquor store. Another I'm there when we kick the shit out of someone who was probably, or possibly, talking to the police. Still another and I'm in on ripping off kids from Jersey trying to buy dope. But there are payoffs I tell myself. I have learned many things, many people, many places. And I have passed most of those on, keeping a few things back that might intrude on my own political hopes. I know, yes, but, I want to get the Dominicans busted, and if I could, the people selling them the weapons down in Virginia, but I don't really want to get a bunch of International Terminal baggage handlers in trouble. They're just trying to fight the good fight, and right now, that good fight needs all the help that it can get.

Are we missing something kid? How come the mick kid gets all the spic names? Gotta remember whose side you're on boy, cause this isn't just a game... but then, you're not looking good? You OK? We could "bust" you and get you a break, no sweat. I mumble that I, "don't know about that." *It always works, it'll buy you a weekend. And hey, that address you got us in Jersey... that's golden man. Good work. Really, you're doing good, we just need the other end of the chain, you know. They ain't really helping your people, you know that, and we really need them. But listen, think about the break, we'll collar you any time you say.*

On a Wednesday afternoon I disappear from the world I have invaded and walk all the way to Brooklyn and through downtown and up Flatbush Avenue. Then I go to the Botanic Gardens. It isn't peak time. The Cherry Lawn and Walk are just green now. Most of the rose garden is past its prime. But it is so quiet here, and I go into the Japanese Garden and go hide up on the hill above the pond, and watch the visitors move below me as the turtles dream on the sun-warmed stones. I fall asleep in the hot calm, waking up just before closing time. And then I walk home to Midwood and drain the water heater with the longest possible shower. Then Kevin pushes his way in and yells "Holy Fuck," and then calls Annie and Margie in and they all stare at my naked body while I attempt to use one hand to cover at least one thing up. "What the fuck have you been doing?" Annie screams, and she shoves the others aside and starts methodically examining the cuts, the bruises, the marks. "You don'na look like a cop with a girlfriend, lad," she says, "You look like shite." Margie is taking pictures throughout, blurry and black and white and two years later they will be the heart of her Thesis Show. Kevin is shaking his head, "I should mail your arse back to Derry," he says, "where at least you might die for a reason."

Yeah kid, yeah. Just stay there. We'll come get you, we'll figure it out. You safe for an hour? Two? "I'm safe for as long as I'm here," I tell them, talking from the only phone we have, traditionally placed at the foot of the stairwell, where the big pillars lead into the never-quite-furnished "Grand Foyer." *Then stay inside, what's the address? We'll send pizza for dinner, how many of you? Yeah, we've got it. Sleep there, we'll pick you up at eight in the morning, and we'll run the show then.* "I just needed to get out for a few," I say. "I just needed..." I didn'a want to sound like a quitter. *No sweat kid, we told you to do this. No big deal at all. Just take care of yourself and sleep.*

Pizza comes from the bar on Foster Avenue, four huge New York pies, along with a case of Molson's, and a giant tub of steamed mussels. My housemates and I sit around the kitchen table, eating without much conversation. "It hasn't been what I expected," I tell them. "What the fuck are you doing?" Kevin asks again. "I cann'a tell you, really..." I say. "Well whatever it be, you better stop," Annie says. "They're working on that right now," I answer. "Who? Whoever sent dinner?" "Yeah." "This is not enough to make up for what they've done to ya." Annie looks at me. She smiles, but her eyes hold an edge of tears. "Hey," I promise them, "I am all OK, just really tired, it will be fine. It will be fine." These are lies, but these are the things you say.

five

The corridors of the Metropolitan Correctional Center are ablaze with the worst of fluorescent lights. Flickering and buzzing with shiny hard surfaces reflecting every visual and auditory switch of 60 cycle alternating current electricity. On top of that assault the air reeks of a tragic mix of sweat and hospital-strength disinfectants. And it is making me sick, as is the first edge of withdrawal, as is fear.

But I have to be here. It is the cover story. So I need to walk these halls at least four times a day, so people will know that I am being questioned. At least for a couple of days – then if I disappear for a week or two – it will all make sense, and I will not only be safe, I will still be useful. And useful is what matters most.

Just tell us everything kid, just talk, we'll record it, we'll decide if it has value. The room is windowless, except for the mirror that lets others watch. The bare table. The old cassette recorder. The overflowing ashtrays, the crowd of Styrofoam coffee cups. It would not look much different if I really had been arrested. Not much different at all. Just tell us the story, every detail you can think of. Give us three days – it will buy you two weeks.

I focus on the little microphone itself. "Sony," is pressed into the black plastic. The chrome grill is dented. A tiny tuft of lint is caught in the corner, stained by the smoke of Camel after Camel and Newport after Newport. I ramble names and faces and street-style descriptions, and places and events, crimes and misdemeanors, parties, sex and drugs. And violence, and more violence, and more violence. In the corner of my right eye I am aware that I am being protected by judicious use of the pause key. The trick to prosecutions based on undercover work is selective memory – backed by the proper use of perjury.

OK, kid, here's the play. We'll bring you to the eight-eight, let you write up what you need to there, then we'll bust you in Midtown South, that'll look best, drag you through that as obviously as possible, right? Then we'll get you to Foley Square. Got to be seen like INS is interested - very interested. Just hang in there. "Can I get coffee, and I need sugar. I need sugar bad." *You look like absolute shit kid, even if you've cleaned up. We supposed to stop at a methadone clinic on the way?* "Fuck you." *No, really, we'll do that if you need it.* "Fuck you." *OK, but I'm guessing you're gonna be a puking mess in five hours.*

When the day's' "interrogations" end they sneak me out in a big black Ford with blacked out windows and switch cars at a strange garage near Sears in Flatbush and drive me home, laden with food - great Chinatown Chinese, then Kosher deli sandwiches from the Lower East Side, then manicotti from Mulberry Street and Cannolis from Le Bella Ferrara. They are trying to make amends, but the food is worthless to me. I am crashing cold turkey.

Where do you wanna go kid? You've got twenty days. Wherever, we'll send you. You just can't stay here. You can't be seen here. But we'll send you anywhere. Pick a spot. "I want to go home, it'll let me recharge." *You can't do that either. We can't let you get into anything there.* "Can't let me get into anything? Are you fucking kidding? You've gotten me into more than I've ever been into in my life." *They do not believe that. I know they know things that I have not told them. I know they know, and they are not saying because I am useful. Exactly what? I'm not fucking sure, but the survival instinct suggests that I stay useful. The room hums around us.* "Can I go to Dublin?" *"How about Cork?"* "I don'na wanna go to Cork," I am begging now. I am getting sick very fast. "I'll stay outside of the city mostly… can you find me someplace to stay in Howth?" *"Howth?"* "Yeah, it's north of the city, on the Irish Sea." *Hang on kid, we'll figure it out. Just hang on. Here's a doctor. He's gonna give you something. It will let you rest.*

They pour me onto an Aer Lingus flight at Kennedy. Down below me, I figure, are one more crate of weapons we have not caught. I smile at that thought. But only for a moment. My skin is crawling, I'm sweating, I'd be sick to my stomach if I had eaten anything in the last two days. They have arranged everything. They have even paid for everything. On the expense reports it will just be listed as "operations related to the cover." They stick traveller's cheques and a big typed information sheet into my pocket, along with a UK passport with one more name. I am whoever they will have me be.

There are moments that contain endless choices, and this, I realize, is one. I have money and clean documents and I really have no reason to go back, or to do anything in particular. This whole experience could be written off as a dream gone completely mad. But I am surprised that when this occurs to me, perhaps as we cross the ocean's midpoint, that I do not let the idea run. I am totally surprised. Instead, I go to the loo, spend ten minutes in the dry heaves, and go back to sleep.

Welcome sir. This guy is a plain clothes Garda and he's met me at the plane door. Welcome, we'll get your luggage and be off. I'm supposed to see that you're all in safe and secure. You'd be one of us? Well, yes, from up north then? And now in America. He says it with a touch of pride. Ireland, even the Republic, is still the Ireland of emigrants, there might be hope on the horizon, but even with the Common Market, things are changing slowly. Success is still measured by victories elsewhere. They found you a grand cottage. Right near the village. Walk to whatever, but there'll be a Rover for you as well. "This is a strange route to Howth," I offer, as we seem to be circling for no real reason. *It would be the route I've been given. No straight lines for you. You're a package we're to be quite careful with.*

Howth is a million miles from Hell's Kitchen. And only the accents hold any similarities. It is hot and dry the first week, but I can barely make it to the local for meals and pints, and stare blankly at awful television from the uncarpeted floor. But then I begin to recover, and in the next week's persistent rains I walk the cliffs, and stroll the shore line, and pick foods from the market, and have gentle and slightly-fictional interactions with those populating the pub in the early evenings.

Slowly life comes back into my brain. But too slowly. On my last afternoon I climb the hill in a steady drizzle and look out over the sea. The lighthouse marks the point below me, and a light fog envelops me, suggesting that I am held safe within the atmosphere of this softer land. Still, the flash of seacoast warning suggests that this cannot last. In the morning the plainclothes Garda will bring me back to the airport. The day after that, or maybe just one further, I will walk out of "federal detention." And then, it will come back at me. Tears now join the rainwater on my face. I must cry now. I'm not sure when I'll get the chance again.

six

On this morning, back in America, back in New York, back in Hell's Kitchen, it snowed. I breathed on the window, it was filthy, and I wiped off the glass with my sweaty t-shirt, and looked out. Big, Hollywood flakes fell down onto the still dark of the far west of Thirty-Ninth Street. Below me the loose valve of the radiator that could not be turned off, hissed steam like a ready kettle.

I turned around, picked up my jeans from the floor and pulled them on, stepped into untied sneakers, and grabbed my hoodie and jacket. Johnny and Cormac and Deaglan were all still completely asleep, and I snuck out the door and tracked my way down the four flights of stairs.

Out on the street I read a quarter to five on a Miller clock in the bar in the building next door, and now, as the sweat on my body turned into ice I walked east until I reached the first place open and selling coffee and sugar, and went in, ordering "coffee black no sugar and two of those with the sprinkles." I stood near the steamed up window. A boy, not over fourteen, played pinball. A radio was tuned to 1010 WINS, "traffic and weather together on the eights." It was 5:08.

A phone booth stood by the curb outside. I went to it, holding the coffee for warmth, and dropped in a quarter and dialed Marcus's office number. "Yo," I said, "Where? When?" "Thirty minutes," he said, "Girl World on Eighth."

I went back inside. Got another coffee. The cup was the traditional New York Greek Diner cup. The coffee was thick and vicious. The snow was getting heavier as the flakes got smaller. I pushed through the cold, a block east and five north to the 24-hour porn store, and slipped inside.

In between the hetero anal videos and the gay shaving videos I told Marcus what I knew, where I was. I gave him the name of a guy at Kennedy who was getting stuff through the fence. I gave him another name, just a first name, of a guy in Jersey who was probably the connection to Virginia guns. I made him give me money so it would look like I had been out "working" if anyone asked. In return Marcus said to be very careful. They were picking up bad chatter. And then we separated, and drifted back out of the place, apart and disconnected. I looked up and down Eighth for maybe a minute. Truck traffic was getting heavy despite the storm. The Trade Center glowed vaguely at the far end of my vision. The sodium street lighting and the pink neon of Girl World made all the colours wrong. I crossed and headed "home."

Walking back, it was still far before seven. It was still dark. It was still snowing. And before I reached Thirty-Ninth I saw the red lights bouncing off the buildings and the falling crystals. I almost began to run towards the lights, but I was not sure exactly how to stay in character, so I moved in the direction slowly and stealthily. I slid along the storefront grates until one cop grabbed me and asked, "What the fuck are you doing here?" But almost instantly, a detective recognised me, and walked with me up the stairs.

Whoever had done this had been fast and deadly. Johnny and Cormac and Deaglan still lay where I had left them, but now each leaked blood from huge holes in their heads. A massive kick through the door, clearly, a very high powered handgun, or two. And it had been over. I stared. I stared for a long time. "Jesus," I kept saying. "INLF?" the detective asked, "Didn't pay for their guns?" "Hard to say," I told him, "but probably, I guess." "You were living here?" "Yeah." "But you don't know?" "No." "You are a fucking skell," he said, "Which side are you on exactly?"

Johnny and Cormac and Deaglan were criminals, of course. Dangerous gun runners. A true part of international terrorism. But still, they were just like me. They were friends even if my job had been to bust them.

"Jesus," I said one more time. Then I tracked my way back down the four flights of stairs, and walked through the snow all the way down to the One-Three on Twenty-First Street, where we were based. I'd let them debrief me. They'd tell me to take a shower. Then they'd give me a week off. Then they'd send me right back in.

seven

"The pockets of our greatcoats full of barley... - No kitchens on the run, no striking camp... - We moved quick and sudden in our own country. - The priest lay behind ditches with the tramp. - A people hardly marching... on the hike... - We found new tactics happening each day: - We'd cut through reins and rider with the pike - And stampede cattle into infantry, - Then retreat through hedges where cavalry must be thrown. - Until... on Vinegar Hill... the final conclave. - Terraced thousands died, shaking scythes at cannon. - The hillside blushed, soaked in our broken wave. - They buried us without shroud or coffin - And in August... the barley grew up out of our grave."

The world closes in fast. In a filthy loft on West 39th Street I had fallen back into my job, and the autumn ended and the cold roared down on the city, chilling the already grey despair of a place and a nation desperately trying to pretend that we are all "doing well." I tried to adjust my attitude just enough. This is a job. I will do my job. I will do just enough to do my job. These were not, however, worlds where straddling the fence works well. Both sides coming at me demanded absolute loyalty. Whatever. I always try to give everyone what they want.

On the first day of snow I barely made it out alive. An accident of timing that rescued me, and I imagined that this would buy me another break, but it only increased my value right here. And so, before I slide out the back of another police facility that evening I find myself on the weight room scale. I struggle through the mental conversion of pounds to kilograms and back til I realize that I have fallen to 127 pounds, the least I have weighed since I was fifteen. And then I make the crucial mistake of looking in the mirror. I shake as I walk the streets trying to decide where to try and sleep this night that will be both warm and "of value," and think that I have achieved the perfect cover: No one will mistake me for anything but a skell on the wrong side of the law the way I look right now.

They'll hide you kid. They'll need to hide you now. Understand, we know this was fucking scary, but it's incredible luck, incredible. They'll take you even deeper. "How the fuck do I get myself back in?" *Who's your guy on Avenue B? Try there.* "He scares the shit out of me, how do I know he didn't just kill these guys?" *I doubt it, we just don't think so. Anyway, you don't have to move in with him, just stay close. And hey, can you connect the dope for us? How many guns are getting traded for smack?* "Give me a few guns and I'll let you know." *Maybe, well, not sure we'd trust you with the evidence right now. There is laughter. One detective gets up and walks away, a locker door bangs. He comes back in and throws a dozen packets of white powder onto the table in front of me. This'll keep you warm this week kid, and share it with someone who can get you information.* "All of you can go fuck your mothers," I spit, *but the packets slip from the table into my pockets.*

By the time this assignment ends after a full year at least eight people will be dead. And I could easily have been number nine twice, at least twice. But I will not be. And because so many are dead, all those who might be able to tell someone that I am not who I claim to be, I will remain the most valuable of operatives. It will be a nightmare without any expected wake up time.

But now I walk toward the World Trade Center. The snow of the morning has given way to rain, though the temperature has barely risen. I finger the wad of bills that are my stake for this game. It has doubled because in the insanity of a multiple homicide morning they have forgotten that they gave me cash just fifteen hours ago. But fuck them. I'm not saying anything. So with extra dollars I slip through the Village and go to John's Pizza and greedily eat a huge pie by myself, making myself as warm as I can. Then I go to a gay bar where I am fairly sure no one will recognise me from any life and shoot up in the bathroom and then nod quietly in the corner. I need to kill the many hours until three or four.

The chart on the wall lists all the possible links. Who are we trying to fill in right now? The lieutenant wants visible progress. His boss walks past this board at least once a week, and a week without additions is a bad week. He bangs his knuckles there, and there, and there. One at a spot between Virginia and New York with a dollar sign and a question mark. Another a line connecting a Dominican drug lord and an INLA "exporter" on the Brooklyn docks. The third is a poorly drawn circle on a line the represents the security fence at JFK. He tells Marco to find a way to work on the money question, but waves his cigarette in my direction and says, Our little junkie needs to get the other two forthwith. I laugh. Police command speak is always funny. "Forthwith" is very funny. *This isn't a joke boy, we've got seven months invested in you and I'm not explaining to some chief how it all vanished into your fucking veins.*

At three-thirty I walk into Tower One and find Óengus who is wiping down the elevator doors. Óengus will get me to Bríghid who I think lives on Third Street around the corner from my target. That's the distance I want. It's also a bed I wouldn't mind climbing into right now. A football sits on the floor by the security desk, and I get Óengus's attention by rifling a kick off the top of the door he is cleaning. "Fuck!" he shouts, but he catches the bounce and heads it back to me. He is from Belfast, from Falls Road, and he's "illegal" but pretty legit. Decent job here on the late night crew. Lives up in Wood-lawn with most of the rest of the northern refugees. But like all of us he knows all kinds of people. We dribble the ball out to PATH Square. "I need

Brighid's number or address," I say, "Shite went down, can't go home." He already knows. He finds a pen in his pocket and scribbles some stuff on a timetable for the PATH trains. "She'll think you're just coming to shag her if you show up before five in the morning," he tells me. "I am coming to shag her," I answer. "Might want to shave first. I've heard she don't like getting scratched down below." "Good advice, I might work on that." I hand him one of the dozen packets. "I don't do this bullshit," he says. "Trade it to Damien for joints," I offer. "You'll make out."

As a kid in school in Derry the priests taught us the poetry of our land. The heroic ballads of the endless battles for lost causes. What, they would ask, gives a man the courage he needs? What arms him for the fight? Who do we remember and why? We sat there in our wool pants and jackets, our shirts and ties, and tried to decide. "They buried us without shroud or coffin..." the poet said that fifty years after the rising. Sometimes it seemed important to die in a way in which you gave everything, so that nothing but your spirit would survive.

The walk across Manhattan, from the Hudson shore to the bulge in the East River, leaves me disoriented and soaked and freezing again. I know Brighid through Óengus, of course, and the parties that artist on the seventy-fifth floor of the north tower throws so that he can watch immigrants of every type strip to their underwear and dance. And I know her from Max's Kansas City where I think she works backstage Friday and Saturday nights. I even know her from Ratner's Kosher on Delancey where she works the lunch shift and effects a surprisingly good Bronx Jewish accent. And I know that she has that milk white skin and flammable red hair of the stereotypical Irish lass. And I know that she is from Armagh, and that being from Armagh, that she suspects that I am not a McDonough from Newry. And I know that this makes this a far more deadly tactic than I should let it become. But I am out of other strategies and I am short on self-preservation skills, and I am desperate to be touched, or at least to be close to a woman. To be warmed by her sight and aroused by her smell and now I have climbed three flights of filthy black and white tiled stairs and I am there and Brighid choses to let me in when I bang on her door. She is wearing white underwear and a torn Ramones sweatshirt and makes it clear that if I need anything other than a couch to sleep on right now I can use my "fuckin' hand, either one, but wipe the fuck up after." And she slams the door that separates the tiny bedroom from the rest of the flat. I pull off wet clothes until I am naked and then stare out the window. The alley slithers among these "old law tenements" in this broken neighborhood. But there is light over there, it illuminates a fire escape and I can see the people's movements animating the shadows. In that apartment might be my man. I imagine that it is, just long enough to allow myself to fall asleep thinking that I have a purpose in this world.

eight

The guy calls himself "The O'Rahilly," and I mean, really, it is a touch over dramatic for a third rate dope dealer and gun runner living above a used TV store on the Lower East Side to name himself after a legendary revolutionary, but we Irish are the poetic type and he fancies himself some kind of liberator. What the fuck. We all need our fantasies.

I have found him in the lowest grade pub on the street and like all who fancy themselves heroes he is easily flattered when you presume his power. "I need to know if they're after me," I tell him. "I ain't done shite to no one, and I could be dead, and that ain't fair." The pub is too hot, the result of desperate efforts to push heat up to the flats above on this bitter day, and I am sweating and the beer is awful. I down three shots of whiskey to get my nerves in check. "Where would you be at now?" "With a neighborhood bird." "Well that can'na be too rough on you, or is your Irish curse worn out?" I smile but don't laugh. "It ain't rough, just not sure it's safe to be out on the streets." "Then stay inside and shag your brains out." "I thought you could help." "Oh," there would be the challenge his ego needed, "Of course I can, it will simply take me a few days. Keep your nob wet and your face out of sight."

The profile says he came here in '72 and that he might have been part of stuff in Belfast. The Brit reports are all over the place. Maybe this, maybe that. He's legal, he's like you, American GI dad, so there's that to remember. He's legal but you are playing that you're not. Busted five times here: assault, assault with a deadly weapon, sale of marijuana, sale of marijuana, assault with a deadly weapon and possession of a firearm. "He been in Newry?" *Don't know.* "Don'cha think that's an important question?" *Not sure where Newry is.* "Fuck, my life's in the hands of morons." I reel off a list of names. "Any of those show up in the dossiers?" *I hate these meetings. Much as I'm scared "out there" I'm more uncomfortable "in here." And doughnuts ain't doing the job my body needs. Especially these doughnuts.* "None with sprinkles?" I demand, fingering all those left in the box. *Why don't you get your rat hands off our food. Jeez. You're just one of them.* "Your choice," I say, "I need a Coke," and I leap up from the chair and bang out of the room and head downstairs to the machine in the locker room. *The locker room is in the basement. It's the middle of the shift. And it is cool and silent. The green lockers lined up, each bearing a sticker reminding us to say, "Police, Don't Move," "freeze" being outlawed as a phrase or relegated to the idiots in the FBI — "freeze or die - FBI," that's what they actually said before they shot each other in the Pierre Hotel lobby last year — asshole "supercops." I'm drifting... Maple benches run between the rows, scratched with absent-minded profane graffiti. I wonder. Could I come into a room like this each day, put on a uniform, go out and answer 911 calls? Isn't that what I should be doing? I'm not gone for long, but they are already worried. Marco is down here, looking for me. Yo man, you OK? you OK?*

I try to keep my nob wet, but Bríghid is not ready yet, or not yet interested. She keeps this a mystery. I settle into watching old movies on channel nine and channel eleven through the slightly blurry thirteen inch television, and try to make myself welcome by cooking for her. I even clean a little. But I get high more. I do venture out, but only in the daylight when everything is busy and I can fade into the crowd, a baseball cap pulled way down over my eyes, and then only to the Met Food three blocks away to find the stuff to cook and the cigarettes to smoke. And then on Tuesday things break. First, a note slides under the door telling me to meet "The O'Rahilly" on Wednesday at four in the back of the pub. Then, after Bríghid drags me out to see a friend in a hospital in Queens, against all my better judgments, and after we eat some bizarre neo-Cuban fish porridge at a very dark restaurant off Jamaica Boulevard, her eyes flashing at me in the light of the red, net-covered table candle, she lets me go down on her in the empty subway car as we screech under the East River. And that unleashes the torrents when we get back to her flat. And that switches my mood almost entirely, in the way it does for boys.

But only briefly. Because now I feel pulled in one more direction. And when I float down to meet the target I am thinking all about how now I indeed might like to just go, to take this woman and run, and that, I already know, is no way to walk into a potential deathtrap.

We think he carries a .45 automatic in a shoulder holster. Does that help? "Who does he know in Ireland?" *He's left-handed.* "Who does he know?" *His family lives in Shankill. We're linking him, maybe to INLA people, not Provos.* "OK. INLA, Belfast, not likely to know much about South Armagh." *If that makes you comfortable, anyway, Marco says his bankers might include a guy we only know as Derek, home-grown American mick on Staten Island. We're working on that. Marco is nodding. I've been digging through ten thousand pages of bank records. We're trying to get you all we can kid, what have you got on this girl?* "The girl ain't no part of this." *Name?* "The girl ain't no part of this." *Oh, it's like that. Listen kid, keep your cock in your pants, you couldn't possibly be doing anything more dangerous than letting that happen.* "Fuck you." *Don't get yourself killed when you're getting off instead of paying attention.* "Yeah, I'll watch that."

"The O'Rahilly" hides me as a "loader." Behind this pub I lift full kegs in and empty kegs out, and then, later on, crates of guns from old station wagons and graffitied Econolines in, and crates of guns back onto shipping company trucks. I barely leave the web of alleys, having figured that I can get from this job to Brighid's flat by climbing two fences and the fire escape. But I am recalling every plate number of every vehicle, and every driver's face. And every third day I go up to the roof and walk three or five buildings west, and climb down. Then I go out into the street, this time though the upstairs entry, that time through the Chinese Take-Out, maybe the next through the faded pink Laundromat having dumped my clothes into the washer on the way, and get myself to one of a dozen spots to meet someone and hand over scribbled notes.

This is it kid. This is it. With this stuff we're tracking it a hundred ways. Which means you probably need to get out soon. "When?" *Don't know. Soon. But first, OK, first... well, we need you to get away and spend a few hours with us. We need you to get involved in something we think is coming.* "What?" *We'll tell you. Thursday at the Ninth?* "Fuck that, I ain't walking into the cop shop down here." *Right, right.* "Make it Central Park, I'd like to get to the park." *We'll set it up. And kid?* "Yeah." *Almost done, but that's when shit goes wrong, so take care of yourself.* "Yeah." *And start slowing down on your habit, you're freaking them out.* "Yeah." *Start slowing down on the girl to — that gets messy.* "Yeah."

The weather is warming up. On gentle early spring mornings, as dawn approaches, I come home and make love to Brighid on the roof. I am trying. I tell her that. I am trying to get myself clean and I am trying to get myself out of the trap I am in. She just says, "Do it if that's what you want, but donn'a be doing it for me." Then we sit naked on our tar beach and stare toward Brooklyn and the sunrise. I sometimes think that the Eight-Eight and my boss are just beyond the river and the Navy Yard on Wallabout Bay. Or I think that I would like this to be real so that I could take this woman and stroll Long Island's beaches with her on a hot afternoon, or I think that my friends, out there in Midwood, are wondering where the fuck I've gone to, though they know that rent checks keep coming. Or I think that way far east, and some north, Ireland sits, green and waiting. And these trysts in the first light are both the saddest part of my day and the one I most look forward to. Brighid, she sits beside me and stares off into the east as well, but I have no idea what she is thinking. No idea at'all.

nine

The spot appears on his forehead, just below the hairline, just to the left of his nose, my left, his right, then a red halo shines behind him, rising on a light from far beyond, the colour of the Pentecost, and then he simply melts.

One moment he is close enough to me that I feel the heat when he exhales, the next he falls completely from my field of vision. Then I hear the first shot, then I hear the second and I dive for the gravelly sand, then I hear the third and my arm catches fire. Maybe there is a fourth or fifth shot. A wave pushes its way in, the incoming tide through Rockaway Inlet and up these salt marshes and bays, and now cold and salty water washes into my mouth.

I slipped out of the neighborhood that Thursday, casually walking Bríghid to Ratner's, like a human, and then finding the Lexington Avenue line and riding north. It was a day of sweet ocean air and I got off at Fifty-Ninth Street, and walked over toward the park, looking at buildings, looking in shop windows, staring at beautiful women, feeling the heat radiate from the concrete as it mixed with the wind crossing the island from the east. I walked around Grand Army Plaza and into the park by the pond and wound my way via Sheep Meadow and Lake and Belvedere Castle and Great Lawn all the way to a small thicket just south of the 86th Street Traverse, where I vanished into the greenery and climbed a stone wall topped by a rusting barbed wire fence, the old easy kind, not the new razor wire, and dropped down into the parking lot of the Central Park Precinct. A rookie cop, all in blue, looked startled, and then we recognised each other. "Holy fuck!" he said. "What the fuck happened to you?" "Lots" "There's this rumor you're doing deep cover." "Maybe." "Either that or you got fired, both are possible." "True." We walked inside together. "Like it?" "Huh?" "Do you like it?" "It's sick shit." "Better than this boring crap." "You're wandering the park all day, you're fucking complaining?" "Doing nothing." "Don't be knocking that." "You always were a lazy little potato eater, why do you get all the breaks?"

We've got six dozen shoulder-fired missiles, we want to know who'll buy them. "What?" *They're obviously not for Ireland, nobody's going after planes or helicopters there.* "We have our limits." *Yeah, well, you do after all. But your pal, what's he called? The O'Rahilly?* "Your accent sucks." *We think he's selling to people in Angola, and maybe Afghanistan, and that mostly funds the rest.* "I thought he was dealing dope?" *That seems like just a cover, or money on the side, it ain't the point.* "I donn'a think I can just show up with seventy-two rocket launchers, unless someone helps me carry them to the subway." *Yeah, anyway, the story is this, a friend of a friend of an old friend has grabbed these from an Army depot. They're all stashed in Coney Island. You can deliver them for, hmmm, we'll figure that out, but this needs to be a single hand-off. They only move from you to the airport guys. They need to get out of the country the minute they start moving, serial numbers and tracing back to guys still in the military and all.* "Sounds fucking crazy." *Sure, Marco looks across the table at me. He is trying to look reassuring but he's scared. Fuck boy, everything you're doing right now is crazier than this.*

I jam my eyes closed as tightly as I possibly can. And now the sea retreats and I can breathe again, and then I begin to hear voices, a full symphony of voices starts to surround me, and Marco and the lieutenant are lifting me up and saying, "Kid, you're alright, kid you're alright." A hand caresses my hair, like I am a wee lad with horrible dreams in the night and they are trying to bring me back to the waking surface.

The O'Rahilly was more greedy than suspicious. Good for me and logical too, since he is really not the target of the day. If he could set up the buyers, I'd get the stuff in a van and I, it had to be me alone, would deliver, and we'd split the cash. A great deal of cash. "But my friends are really scared," I told him. "They're way the fuck over their heads on this. They don't trust nobody and they want this shit on the first plane out. Gone." It took three weeks to get the details right. Three weeks of absolute fear while I also tried to cut back on the medicine – twenty four hours between, thirty, thirty-six, forty-eight, careful, stay sane. I couldn't cut back on Bríghid though. She had become the only thing I actually had.

What do you have? We're in the corner of a Chock Full o' Nuts, standing at a counter. "By boat apparently, they want to take this straight in through the fence from Jamaica Bay." *That's weird, ain't it?* "Yeah, but there are rumours, that's probably your fuck up." *Not mine scumbag.* "Maybe not you personally, but you know. They're afraid of the truck gates with something worth this much." *So where?* "Broad Channel, deep late." *That's a shit place to try and cover you, I don't like it.* "Not much choice now." *You know who's coming? Any ideas?* "One guy from Belfast, looks like my brother, works for British Airways I think. He hangs in back of the pub a lot. He's not the brains, just the connection." *Trust them?* "I don't even trust you." *Listen kid, whether this goes good or bad, it's got to look like you've run. You've got to be out of here within 24 hours and on the way to Ireland. A month off free. We'll have papers for you.* "I'm tired." *Yeah, yeah you are.*

I get my eyes open and look down. The corpse at my feet was, just seconds before, that guy who looked almost exactly like my brother, lost in those Vietnamese jungles, trying to be an American in his way, in his time. "Pro carissimo salutares hostias immolavit amico." Why exactly did we want to be Americans anyway? It seems increasingly less healthy. This guy had so reminded me of home, I had pretended he was a friend in a way that convinced me, if not – I'm guessing now – him. All that was dissolving now, and I see the nine millimeter spilling from the back of the belt, two fingers still wrapped to it, and I watch Danny grabbing it with latex-gloved hands. And now my eyes take in just enough more, the three guys who now lie dead at the waterline, in the huge and quickly deflating raft with the massive outboard. I don't know any of them. My hand is still clutching the keys to the supposedly stolen construction company van that sits above us near the blue house over there. If the plan had gone right I'd have swapped the keys for the money and taken the A Train back to Broadway-Nassau. But it has not gone right. My hand is still clutching the keys and my hand is dripping wet. I'm assuming that it is water, but I suppose that it really is not.

I have asked Bríghid to come away with me. To take the month off and come back home. I tell her that things will be crazy for a bit but then it will be OK. But she just shakes her head, that hair flying and thrilling me. She has known boys like me all of her life, she knows that it is never really OK, no matter who I might actually be. "Run if that works for you," she says, "If I want to be found when ya get back, you'll be able to find me."

Shit kid, hold still while we get this bandage on. Sorry kid, we weren't trying to nail you, but it was a damn close shoot. Just grazed anyway, there's nothing in there. Paramedics are all over the place. The snipers are coming down to the beach from their hiding spots. The beach is full of people and lights, sirens are screaming across the causeway, echoing off the edges of the bay. We'll get you to the hospital, then, anyway, we've got a passport for you and everything else. You did great kid. Time to sleep it off. "This wasn't the plan." *Fuck kid, did you really think there was a plan? They try to laugh. A blanket is thrown over me. You're shaking kid, relax, it's over now.*

The sun is just starting to rise and I walk up from the water. I look west and the tops of the Trade Center flicker silver touched with gold at the far end of this world. We ride to the nearest hospital, wrapped as if I am once again under arrest. No chances now. A nurse washes me and I change clothes. They have brought me new everything. I'm grateful. And now Marco drives me to JFK in an old Chevy passing me this and that. An Irish passport now, Ruarí MacSweeney, "Jesus fuck, who came up with that?" "Donegal name, no? They're trying to be accurate for ya." "Fuck." "It's just for a month. Then we can get you back." "And then I do what?" "Depends on how our story sells on the streets." "It's not up to me?" "It never is kid. It never really is."

Before I get on the plane I call Kevin at home. "They're sending me to Ireland for a month – I'll send you guys postcards." "Where the fuck have you been, and you sound like worst shite than before." "Yeah, but I'm OK." "No, you're not." "All right, but Dublin will cure what ails me." "Maybe." "Here's hoping."

It is a complicated story to sell, and we need to keep you valuable. We're making you "Assistant Liason to the Garda Síochána," six months or so. You don't really need to do nothing. "What if I don't want to stay valuable." *We need you kid.* "Yeah." *Life ain't bad there is it? Didn't think so. Oh kid...* "Yeah." *Got some bad news.* "What?" *That girl? Someone might of thought she set you up.* I'm silent. In this little flat in Dublin I put the phone down, but the sound comes through anyway. *Found her body in the East River, sorry kid.*

I leave the phone where it is. I can hear the voice calling my name. I walk to the window and light a cigarette. The Irish sky is turning from blue to rain, as it often does.

The Third Man

When you do things you shouldn't do you should do them alone. Every accomplice multiplies the risks a hundred fold. Everyone, no matter how much you might trust them – believe in them – think of them like a fucking brother. It does not matter. One person committing a crime in the dark is very likely to get away with it. With two it's fifty-fifty, with three it's just a matter of time before they show up at your door.

Ocean's Eleven? Bollocks to that mate. Someone will talk. You'll all be nailed. They always do.

So if you're gonna nick a car from the carpark near a far beach in the west of Donegal on a Saturday morning because you've ended up there and you need to get back one way or a t'other, well, it should be you and just one. We knew that, but then, who'd we leave? Just wouldn'a worked, ya know.

I had suggested just walking back. Three days? Maybe just two and a half. But there was little ambition for that and Donal had come up lame from stepping on something in the sea anyway so that wouldn'a worked a 'tall unless – and Thomas and I considered this – we found a telephone and called for an ambulance for him, and disappeared. But loyalty matters, and that wouldn'a be the kind of story you'd want getting round about you.

We all had our rules. I wanted a Ford or a Vauxhall cause I knew how to start both with ease. Thomas said we couldn'a take nothing with toys in it, you wouldn'a do that to a kid. Donal wanted comfort, he thought a camper, but I would never take someone's house, even if it's a rolling one. That would'a been too close to being an imperial, and I'd been raised better.

In the end we snatched a Cortina about a half an hour after some banker-looking type and his too-young-looking shagbag got out of it. We headed east. Me at the wheel. Thomas riding shotgun – an American term we loved – and Donal lying and whining in the back. We crossed the mountains, cutting through the center of the county much as we could, soaking in the sights like a family on holiday. Didn'a even need petrol to get us back to Castleforward where we left it behind a huge oak, and walked the last ten miles, carrying the limping lad between us.

Donal confessed, of course. Not to police. No never that. But at Confession. He was in pain. He thought he had caused the crime. He needed a way back to grace. And all three of us got belted by the priests in school, all week long.

Never sure if the punishments were for stealing the car, or running from town in the first place, or for Donal telling tales, or for Thomas and me not confessing our own sins.

priceless

They said money was easy in Dublin. There'd be Americans there and if you begged on the Ha'penny or on the O'Connell Street Bridge, you'd collect enough in any afternoon to take care of the night. But back then there were more poor kids from everywhere in the country, especially those running from the towns out west that had failed a hundred and fifty years before, and those fleeing Belfast, than there were Americans coming to find their roots. And the rest of Europe was still discovering Paris and Rome and London, and had not yet reached out to the edges. And Dublin itself was still a fairly poor place, the promises of European socialism still waiting just over the horizon.

The ambitious or the very hungry staked out spots in the early morn, hoping those tramping to work would throw coins their way. They rarely did. The others crowded in around half ten, tattered, dirty, trying to dig out of an accelerating cycle of drugs. Crossing the Liffey in 1980 was to wade through a swamp of smells, stale weed, urine stained denim, and ancient sweat.

On a Wednesday night Caitlin and Michael appeared in our flat just up the hill from the Brazen Head and announced a mission of good will. I was ready to be done with Dublin, alternately plotting escapes to the States, or to an art school in Strasbourg, or back to the north, but we really didn't have it bad. Six of us shared this old place. We all, more or less, had work. Food, beer, soft drugs, and even sex were plentiful. We may not have been making progress, but it wasn't a bad place at'all.

Michael worked for a grocer, and had liberated a few cases of stout, along with piles of bread and a load of cheese. He claimed it had been "obtained" from the lorries of suppliers, not his employer, a distinction that seemed meaningful at the moment. Caitlin declared, "The people need food!" and we all joined this instantaneous revolution.

As darkness dropped across the city we loaded backpacks and began a route crisscrossing the river, going cold doorway to cold doorway, handing out our gifts, sometimes disguising our accents as Australian, "G'day mate!" sometimes as Americans, "How ya doin' fella," sometimes as Parisians, "Bon nuit mon frere." We spent perhaps two hours as angels of mercy, because, whatever the circumstances, you share what you can, even if what you can share is not really yours.

At eleven or so we had five cans of beer left. We sat down on the kerb opposite St. Stephen's Green and pierced the tops. "That was a fine night," Sile said, "A fine night." A full moon was climbing into the black sky. We drained the cans and headed back home.

heat

The day was too hot. That rarely happened, so we were unprepared. It was not a city with pools or even hoses for the watering of grass. Really, except for the hill by the walls, there was no grass back then. Not on our side of the river.

The haze turned the hills to the west into a soft grey cloud and we sweated simply standing on the pavers, even on the shaded side of the street.

Deirdre stepped from her front door and began a story of swimming in a huge pool in London with her uncle. "That would be class," Malachi said, but Niall just told her to "stop being a lying tosser." And we sat silently for more minutes.

Then Cahal's Da walked down the street from the pub, lugging a long black coil over his arm, and pushed open the door of his house and vanished inside. We looked toward it curiously. Cahal's Da had never had a job, but he always seemed important to everyone, so we wondered. And yet, we were fully unprepared when the huge spray of water erupted from the second floor window ten minutes later, soaking us, cooling us, making us all shriek.

We played for hours. Stripped to our jockeys and drawers, dripping and delirious. Until we shivered under the sizzling sun.

"We have no prairies," he is quoting the Nobel Laureate, "To slice a big sun at evening. Everywhere the eye concedes to. Encroaching horizon." "Yes," I agree, "he did write that indeed." We have been pounding the pints for hours now. The pub is full, and noisy, but we sit isolated at the center. Arsenal played the early game and here the rain is slashing down and while my computer is here, is on, is wirelessly connected, and I will be sure to tell anyone asking that I am working on something that must be in Monday morning, I have added but seventeen words since I got here - I glance at the time, and mumble "holy fuck" - five hours ago. "You grow up burnin' the turf on the hearth?" he asks. "That I did, but ahh," I pause and thicken the expected accent, "You know us northerners, primitives all." He smiles, gets up to get more Guinness. It is his turn. I type five sentences in while the barkeep watches the ale settle, then delete two. "But you know the prairies over there in the states too." He is back, banging the glasses on the hard polished wood. "Aye, laddy," I croon, "I have crossed the Great Plains, I have sailed the Great Lakes, I have climbed the great towers." I pause, drink, whisper, "They do not know about digging up ancient swamps and burning them for warmth in America." "They have always had oil in America," he returns in the same conspiratorial voice. "They have always had everything they want in America." "But you came back." I nod. I drink. I nod again. Liverpool is winning. It is raining across the Irish Sea as well, the camera lenses display the wind driven water, making the match seem more like memory. Outside the very air seems to have turned sea green under this autumnal downpour. "The scrotum tightening sea," I say, "Ah, Joyce," he slurs. Then, "Joyce never came back, why did you?" "You can see too far in the States," I tell him. "You can see so far ahead of you that you forget to look in back of you." "And that would be no way for an Irish lad to live," he either states or asks. I am not sure. We both take long drinks. "No, I suppose it is not."

walls

The street is as filthy as it is abandoned. The clouds foretell rain. And the wind bristles, sending shivers along my spine.

If you walk the "peace walls" of Belfast you can smell the failure. The failure of community, of leadership, of religion, of humanity. It is all written beneath the grubby graffiti on the cold concrete that long ago replaced the simpler fences, and then began to climb higher. Because once you build a wall, you quickly discover that it cannot truly be high enough.

I grew up alongside the seventeenth century's attempt to separate Catholics and Protestants. Those walls are massive. Carved stone. Incredibly thick. And were powerfully armed. You can walk along the top of these walls today, Europe's last truly walled city, and look down on what was once a Catholic ghetto and what was once a battlefield where the native soldiers of Ireland almost drove the English into the sea, but not quite.

These twentieth century dividers in Belfast and Derry are less picturesque, and when, someday, they are gone, they will be no more mourned than the Berlin Wall, but like that structure, perhaps we should preserve big sections so that future generations will know.

Walls do not work. Walls are proof only of the fact that you have run out of ideas. It does not matter if the intent is to keep people in (Berlin), keep people out (the US/Mexico Border), or keep people apart (the north of Ireland or Palestine). Behind every wall anger and frustration build and resentment festers and dangerous myths grow. Humans do not like boxes unless they are free to go in and out. Of this there is no doubt. And humans separated by walls simply will not learn to get along. This is also true.

The street is as filthy as it is abandoned. And now the clouds have started spitting cold water. I have walked from one rusting "peace gate" toward another, sticking to the Catholic side, since walls force that type of decision. Over there is grim poverty. Over here is the same.

daybreak

I am up early and wandering the city on one of the last chill days before spring truly breaks. I could not sleep this night. I had started dreaming moments from my time in Dublin at the end of the 1970s, and though, yes, most moments of that time would make excellent, even extravagant dreams, those were not the moments my brain chose to replay.

So I arose. Made coffee in absolute silence. Filled the kind of giant thermal cup Americans love to drive with. And set out from Aidan's, walking up Baggot Street, looping the lock on the Grand Canal with swans fishing in the first light and water pouring over the gates, and then north toward the city center.

Dublin awakes more slowly than most of the world's big cities. Oh, certainly, there are the up-and-comers in their almost tailored suits heading to banking jobs tied to London, Frankfurt, Paris, and Rome. There are the corporate transplants from the US sometimes even running the streets at this hour. But it is still a sleepy city, with very light traffic, uncrowded footwalks, and even the lorries with morning shop deliveries only just beginning to roll. That Irish pace of life, so derided by the English and the Americans, well, perhaps they should calm down a bit and try it.

Now I circle St. Stephen's Green and the early blooms, wet with the dew, lift their smells to me, and then I stride along Grafton Street as lights begin to flicker on behind the still locked doors of the expensive shops. Brown-Thomas has a slightly perverted Barbie theme going on. Across the way Marks & Spencer promises a great sale.

By the time I reach the Liffey the metropolis has stirred itself, and cars and vans fill the Quaysides, while a gaggle of Spanish tourists floods past, fully backpacked. They must have just hopped off the airport coach. Before I cross the bridge to O'Connell Street a shop window offers me as much alcohol as anyone could possibly consume mixed with the gifts – stuffed bears and all sized boxes of chocolates – that will then be needed to apologize to the woman in my life.

I will need to apologize, obviously, but not for that, and not yet. I will let her sleep in, and wait another hour to call.

When I reach the spike, where Nelson's statue once stood proclaiming British rule, I can tell that it will be a perfect day. When I reach the Abbey

---

Theater I pull the mobile from my pocket, and press the number three.

"You awake?" I ask. "Where the fuck are you?" "It's a perfect, perfect, lovely day," I say. "You know you scare the shit out of me." "Come meet me. We'll ride the DART to Howth and play by the sea." "Aren't you going to the library to work?" "It is a perfect day." "What did your mother say about "your father's work habits"?" But she says that with a laugh.

"It is a perfect, perfect, lovely day," I repeat.

"Give me an hour and some," she tells me. "Meet me by the bridge. Have coffee for me." I say, "Absolutely," and lean back to stare at the deep blue sky.

borderline

Newtownhamilton sits hard on the now invisible border, where County Armagh meets County Monaghan in the steep green glens of the Fews above Carlingford Lough. On one side of this tiny place where the cattle market comes weekly the sign says "Fáilte go dtí An Baile Úr / Welcome to Newtownhamilton" but at the other end of the high street the sign reads only, "Welcome to Newtownhamilton." Even in a place this tiny the lines remain drawn, though if you sit in the mid-day dim of the Central Bar sipping your pint, there is no evidence of threat.

But up the road, between here and the old church and the cattle market itself is the barracks. Big and green and bristling with cameras and antennas. Mostly empty now, mostly quiet, where once it was filled with British Army soldiers watching the border and trying to track who was carrying what from there to here.

Bad things happened in Newtownhamilton. Terrible things. You cannot really imagine it as you look around. It is a postal card village, Brigadoon if you must continue to confuse Celts. Still, things happened, as they always do in occupations. The last time I was here in this town... we will not talk about that now, but let it stand that I was not a tourist here to view the gentleness of the copses of trees that stand out among the pasturelands.

But now I am, at least in part. And after a pint or two my friend Seamus and I return to a field beyond his new home and play football with his kids at the base of those beautiful hills. He tells me that his children do not really understand what "that fort" was for. I suggest that he save that information until they are much older.

Still, late on this night we will go for a walk and smokes, and wander the hills and fields, back and forth for hours across that old line on the map, just because now we can do it slowly, and we can see this place without the lenses of fear.

Iarnóin

We sit in the sunlight, splayed across the grass and the clover that it ruffled in rich patterns by a confused breeze from the sea, and breathe in each other. The clouds anchoring the southern horizon threaten us with chill rain but here that airflow holds them at bay, letting our local star warm us.

That same breeze carries the smells of salt, of fish, of seaweed, of our wooly farm animals, and of our richest, densest earth and makes a hushed duvet of them, overlying us, wrapping us, telling us that this moment should be held.

Beneath this quilt she assures me that I am alright, without saying a word. And with my own deep silence, I try to tell her exactly how hard I am trying.

flight

If I had known how the nightmares would come I would not have gone to Belfast that day. If I had known how ghosts might leap from the edges of my vision when I get tired I would have crossed the border that Easter weekend someplace other than the town with the barracks. If I had known how many nights I would walk beaches and quaysides and city streets waiting for the rescue of dawn I might not have volunteered to be in deep cover when the targets became faces that were familiar. If I had ever imagined how much I would miss the hills and cliffs and valleys and voices of the north coast, I just might not have traversed the ocean again at twenty-three. If I had ever thought that I would not see my brother again, I surely would have begged him to not go be an American soldier when he did not have to. And if I could have realized how much worry I created for my Ma, I would have tried to be a different kind of child.

In just hours I will be in the air. Suspended between two homes and two lives. The sun will ignite the green of the fields below. And then it will glisten off the rolling Atlantic waves. I will stare out the window of seat 34K feeling sad, feeling hopeful, feeling regret, feeling slightly lost in a world that has let me see the fullest range of its possibilities.

And sometime before we break across the coast of eastern Quebec and the New World forest spreads out below us and the flight attendants come down the aisle with tea and coffee and desserts, I will tell myself that I can only change the future. And that, like any good Irish kid, I still believe in heaven, I still believe in redemption, and I still believe in magic.

Justice

There was this fortnight long ago, one of those rare escapes desperate adults would try to arrange for us, and me and Colin and Donal went to stay with a cousin of Donal's out near Sligo on a farm where there was no electricity but we could swim in the ocean and help cut sod from the bog and haul it back to dry with a cart pulled by a donkey and all you heard at night was the surge of the Atlantic onto the beach and sounds of insects. A time away that rescued a year.

And then, later on, Donal ran off with dangerous people and never came back. Until this week.

I do not know what Donal did, what he might have been involved in. Might it have been horrible? Surely. The world was filled with awful crimes then, as now. I met him again almost a decade later at the start of 1985 in New York's Hell's Kitchen. We had taken opposite paths to this moment, and we both knew more about each other than we would admit to anyone else, which somehow, I really do think, worked to both of our advantages. Bonds formed in childhood are crucial and sacred, and we would not break them.

People, by which I mean people I worked for back then, thought that Donal knew about the bomb at Jordanstown, and maybe, maybe he did. There was a captain who really wanted him to somehow have been involved in the murderous Christmas bombing of Harrod's, but that made no sense to me, the timelines just did not match. Still, 1982, 1983 were ugly, ugly years, and there was more than enough guilt to go 'round. In New York City, in Ireland, around the globe there just was not much of a moral compass. In Central America Ronald Reagan was arming right-wing nun-raping counter-revolutionaries and in the Middle East he was handing weapons of mass destruction to both Iran and Iraq. In Afghanistan the Russians were killing radical Islamists while the CIA was arming them. Things were brutal in China and Southeast Asia. The Basques were setting bombs off once a week. Ulster was just one disaster among many while Reagan and Thatcher battled with the Russians over Poland. As Donal himself said, "It takes something special just to make the papers."

Still, something had happened. There were all kinds of lists back then in the hands of the Army, the MI-5, and the RUC, and probably most of our pictures were on one or another, but Donal, well, it was somehow thicker than just that, and he remained an OTR, an On-The-Run, someone who dared not step back into the territories of the United Kingdom no matter what. Instead he stayed in New York, working construction, working in pubs, becoming older and wider and quieter and more and more legitimate, even if never really legal, until a lifetime of Guinness and cheap American beer and good whiskey and probably dark fear caught up with him and a heart attack crushed him on a Brooklyn subway stairwell.

Somewhere south of London this month Tony Blair's people are shredding and burning papers. They are in Belfast too. And surely they are in comfortable homes across the British landscape. These are the old MI-5 officers and operatives, who are sweating out the possibility of discovery in the twilight of their years. Almost 18 years ago an inquiry was begun into the MI-5 - that British internal spy agency - and the Royal Ulster Constabulary, the former Protestant police force of Northern Ireland, and their collusion in myriad murders with "Loyalist Paramilitaries." Well, I suppose, they were all on the same side "back then," they were all trying to keep the six northeastern counties of Ireland in the United Kingdom and out of the hands of the "Popist Republicans" in Dublin. And after 18 years and piles of proof, almost nothing will happen to any of these perverters of justice. They keep their rich government pensions and sit in their country cottages in quiet retirement and Blair's government gives them back the papers proving their guilt so they can wipe away the evidence, just as the Brits continue to ignore the piles of arms in the hands of gangs of thugs like the Ulster Defense Force and the Ulster Volunteer Force. The IRA must disarm, of course, but not their equally dangerous opponents. OTR Republicans can only return in coffins but guilty British politicians get knighted.

I do not know what Donal did. But as I stood in the cathedral in Derry and said the funeral mass for my friend from long ago, I thought that reconciliation cannot come without equal justice. Either we can all repent and come home or we all must be exiled or tried. There is either retribution or redemption. We all must make the choice.

Donal's mother comes up to me later. "He was happy in New York? Truthfully?" I touch her hand. "He was a happy man," I said, "He had many friends, he was loved." "Aye," she says, "but he would have liked to see this place one more time." "Aye," I agree, "That he certainly would'a."

Easter

"Liberation comes hard," he says. He is very old. Very. Old enough to almost remember, or, if not that, to have been raised on the first-hand tellings. He is on his fourth pint, so is this truth? It does not matter. It is the truth even if it might not be his truth. "We are all in this together," he also says, "it is all of our story."

His father was burned to death by the Black and Tans when he was less than two when they set a rural cottage afire. An uncle spent twelve years in British prisons, here and over there. He spent time in the Borstal at Hollesley Bay that Brendan Behan would make famous. He lost a son to a premature bomb explosion in Belfast in 1976. And yet, he sighs the deep sigh of ancient lungs that have breathed a lifetime of peat and tobacco smoke, he still finds himself living in a place "ruled by a fuckin' queen."

He looks at me. I am not at all sure that he can see much at this distance, but, he looks at me. "You've run away to America," he says, "Did you find freedom there? Did you find what you wanted?" "A different kind of freedom," I answer, "and I've found lots of things but not quite what I need." He nods, barely, almost imperceptibly. Takes another drink. His great grandson lights another cigarette for him, and he takes it in hands the colour of an apple core left on the table all day. "So you are back, and you, and all of you will keep up the battle."

We won't really. We are a generation changed. Are we Europeans? Not quite. Not the way the French and Germans or even the Irish in the Republic are. We are too far on the edges of the world for that. But "fight" is no longer in our hearts. "Wait" is the better word. We are waiting for political borders to vanish. We are waiting for old enemies to die away. We are "culturalists," not "nationalists."

None of us will say that right now, though. We can barely even think it as we sit here, on this eve of the Easter, thirty hours before the 91st anniversary of the Easter Rising. After all, we can only think that way because of the long fight of our ancestors – our ancestors embodied in the old man sitting here and his stories.

The great grandson whispers to him that it is time to go. He smiles, as much as he can, and holds his glass up. "To the Irish Republic," he announces, "To the patriots of the Easter Rising." We bang our pints together and repeat his words. "Take care of yourselves lads," he says, "Drink hearty and safe home."

Five minutes after he leaves someone switches the radio from RTE na Gaeltachta to the alt rock of 2fm. The noise level rises. Three women, too young for any of us, stop by and attempt to chat. Michael says something about buying a new car. We have shifted from the old Eire to the new so quickly, but before I go fully along, I consider how hard it is to fully understand the sacrifices that make Easter holy.

Skinnydipping in Ireland

"I'm not," I say, "but you could get naked and swim." She just looks at me. "It's a long way down, but we'll just go to the edge so you can see." We are walking the coast of Dublin Bay from Sandycove to Killiney and she has already nixed leaping in at The Forty Foot. "You swim here, don't you?" "Oh yeah, but I prefer it from May on." "Is it much warmer then?" "The water, not a'tall, but the air is, so you thaw much faster." And now, past Dalkey, past a lunch of soup and cheese and stout, we are walking down the hill to the water. "This is a Clothing Optional Swim," the graffiti says as we cross the DART tracks. The old man of the rocks appears, "Going in today lad?" He asks, "Nice to see you back." "If you are up here," I ask him, "who will pull me out?" He laughs. "I've had congestion in my chest all winter, can't go in, can only watch." I tell him to get himself well and he climbs the path and disappears. "You know him?" she asks. "Well, certainly, we've chatted many times." "You actually know these random people on a weird path to a cold, nude beach?" "It's a small country." "You are all crazy." "That we must be." The sky above is grey, we hold umbrellas begged from another old acquaintance, a barman in Dalkey who picked two for us from the "forgotten by tourists" bin. The rain adds weight to the smell of the gorse flowering the hillside. Below us the Irish Sea breathes in and out, rising and falling as earth and moon spin in concert.

Shelter

I dreamed there were islands north of us. Not so far as the Faroes, but north, like Scotland has the Orkneys. And not while I was asleep. These were the dreams from before sleep came or when I'd lie there in the dark waiting for morning or sometimes when I couldn't really sit in school anymore but couldn't get up either and so I had to let my brain travel.

I dreamed there were islands north of us and they were made of green hills rising from white beaches from a stormy Atlantic that faded to calm blue on the leeward side. Where the terrace houses were painted in bright colours like the best villages and white-sailed schooners still came in from hard days at sea and we ran to school as Cathedral bells rang and sheep bleated far off in the distance as they moved to their day's pastures.

Over years I filled in detail after detail. It became its own Irish and Catholic nation, Oileáin Maidin, the Morning Islands. Free and at peace and stuck back in time in some deep way where all of the stories of the Great Uncles and their childhoods would still be true. I knew it took two hours to drive the main island north to south but less than one to cross east and west and that fifty other islands, ranging from three miles square down to a single lonely house filled the waters surrounding us, joined by tiny wooden ferries that puffed smoke from black stacks amidship. I knew the flag was green with the gold harp on it, like the one that flew over the GPO in 1916, but that the lower half was the blue of the ocean. I knew it was a place where the nights were quiet and the kids were always safe.

I dreamed there were islands north of us and that was a place that I could hide. Those lands rescued me on many days and even more nights before they vanished in the mists of adolescent reality, though sometimes, just sometimes, as I struggle from sleep on a dark winter morning, I can still look down my Morning Island street toward my own safe harbor.

Poetry

Clouds run in from the west and then break apart. Huge swaths of sun falling across the fields as if God were operating the spot light for this scene in our lives. The wind off the sea is cool but the day is shockingly warm and we are carrying beer and whiskey and cheeses and brown breads and soda breads and strange seafood pastes from Tesco and a tin or two of oysters and competing at remembered verses of poetry and singing a wild mix of songs from long ago.

Above the beach at Culdaff we come into the circle. You would not know it but for the stories. Just four upright stones and rubble in a sheep pasture near the edge of Inishowen. Three thousand years ago, maybe four, ancient Celts prayed here, and celebrated, and buried their dead. Humans had moved to this island three or four millennia before that, moving north and west across the continent and the islands torn from its fabric by the violent ocean. By the time they raised the stones in this spot where the morning sun would first strike, they had an ancient culture, deep mythologies, and a history of survival despite all odds.

There is much I could be concerned with this day. There is horrible news back in America – another random mass shooting. There is the work I am here to do. There are the things I need to write. And there are the plans to return to the university that pays me. But Colin and Brendan and Thomas's younger brother Michael thought we should pull one of our childhood "escapes" at least one more time. And I could not have agreed any faster.

Back then our runs to quiet valleys, empty beaches, long-forgotten churches, and ancient ruins had kept us together and safe and sane when our world felt most dangerous and most beyond our understanding. We fled to be alone. We fled to need nothing but each other. We fled into a more heroic past. We fled into myth.

"Had I the heavens' embroidered cloths, Enwrought with golden and silver light, The blue and the dim and the dark cloths. Of night and light and the half light, I would spread the cloths under your feet: But I, being poor, have only my dreams; I have spread my dreams under your feet; Tread softly because you tread on my dreams." Colin chants Yeats in a thick rhythm.

And Brendan counters with Kavanagh, "You clogged the feet of my boyhood, And I believed that my stumble, Had the poise and stride of Apollo, And his voice my thick tongued mumble. You told me the plough was immortal! O green-life conquering plough! The mandril stained, your coulter blunted, In the smooth lea-field of my brow."

I look at the sky, framed by these altar stones, take a large drink of Black Bush and pass the bottle. Then I smile at my oldest friends, and pull Seamus Heaney from memory. "The annals say: when the monks of Clonmacnoise. Were all at prayers inside the oratory. A ship appeared above them in the air. The anchor dragged along behind so deep. It hooked itself into the altar rails. And then, as the big hull rocked to a standstill, A crewman shinned and grappled down a rope. And struggled to release it. But in vain. 'This man can't bear our life here and will drown,' The abbot said, 'Unless we help him.' So. They did, the freed ship sailed and the man climbed back. Out of the marvelous as he had known it."

We eat and drink in the full glory of northern spring. We are not where we were. But we remain exactly who we were. And that is precious.

Degrees of Damage

It is a place of red hand flags and heroin and thick Protestantism, the politics not the religion really, except that the religion is in so deep, and the new Sainsbury's and the new cinema really can't cover it up no matter how much the district council talks of new jobs or how many kids go to the integrated college, because, well, that's the top and the top doesn't tell you much. Never has.

So the Reverend Paisley will make phone calls and will pretend that he prays for the lost child. And Sinn Fein will insist that this proves that they are not the bad people here. And in houses across this "province," if it is that, or this "occupied territory," if it is that, because, holy fuck, it is both and neither and we all know that, more will stoke their offspring with hatred than will stoke them with compassion, all the while blaming "them" – Taigs, Proddies, Brits, Provos, Orangemen…

Michael McIlveen went to see a film on Sunday. He was fifteen and, well, I do not know. I did not know him. But I was fifteen once, and an angry fifteen at that, in an angry place, and fifteen-year-old boys run in packs, and they say things, and they challenge each other. It is what they do, what I did, what you did. It is one way we test the world. So, no matter that his family says he was just a "wee quiet one," and, yes, he may have been, as I said, I don't know. It does not matter. Was he quiet? Was he angry? Was he quiet at home but boisterous in his group? We know lads like that, do we not? It does not matter.

Michael McIlveen went to see a film on Sunday in Ballymena. An ancient town where the bells of ancient churches rhyme through stone streets and echo across the land. A Catholic kid among Catholic kids in a Protestant town. A kid in a place people have divided because they like power and privilege and because they do not care. And perhaps, just perhaps, at the cinema he said something, or someone said something. Things are always being said, but we all know that here they do not need to be.

Michael McIlveen went to see a film on Sunday in Ballymena and sometime after the film was over he was chased down a street and beaten with a bat and stomped by other boys, damaged boys, because he was Catholic, because the Reverend Paisley likes power, because Tony Blair will spend billions of pounds on Iraq but cannot be bothered with his "province," because the London literati announced last year that The Troubles were over, because the world has grown tired of this, because not enough people will stand up and say "stop."

Michael McIlveen went to see a film on Sunday in Ballymena and now his family will bury him in the cocoa-coloured soil of the north of Ireland, and the rains will fall, and the bells of ancient churches will rhyme through stone streets and echo across the land. Everyone on the island has expressed their regrets – as I am sure they should.

In London the Prime Minister could only say, "My legacy is a fourth term for Labour." The Queen said nothing at all.

This Dublin Night

The busses have stopped running and so has the DART and I could grab a taxi but that seems indulgent and unnecessary. It is warmer than it might be and though the fog is thick it is not raining and above there is even the slightest hint of moonlight and I really do not have that far to go and nothing urgent in the morning.

Walking is the great equalizer. It is the human mode, used since we first dropped from the trees in Africa. And night is a vast sea with the strongest of tides, it is not the human time. It is when we hide or when we cower behind whatever artificial lighting we can muster, from the ancient open fire to the grating non-colour of the modern streetlamp.

You can only learn a place by walking. That is why the places you know from childhood are closest to you. And you can only know a city intimately by walking through its night. Then you see the secrets as the lighted rooms reveal themselves and the darkened shops speak without the affected accents they strive for while open. You see the cars of the residents and their trash, and without the purposeful sounds of planned life you can hear every argument, every cough, and even the cries.

Tonight I cross the south side of Dublin, neighborhood by neighborhood. From tiny homes to huge houses to fake castles to streets of those ugly 70s flats that replaced beautiful Georgian Colonial structures at the height of our hatred for all things English. The big spaces in most homes are dark. Blue television light flickers in some bedrooms. Six people sit by computers. One woman and three men stand naked by their respective windows. A couple snogs in a doorway. The sounds of sex echo from one house, but they are hard to place exactly. One Seat, two Volkswagens, and a Renault drive past. In the Renault a couple sit close. In the Seat a woman looks scared.

What is home for right now starts to come into view after an hour. The small high street and the Green appear ahead, vulnerable and soft in their silence. I think that I surely wish I could really afford to live here, because, yes, it is great. But then, even if temporary, it is one more gift. One more place which I have learned.

I turn onto my street. Three houses off the corner a baby screams in a gently lighted room painted the blue of the warmest summer sky. The mother rocks the child as she sings, "I love my love and well he knows. I love the ground whereon he goes. If you no more on earth I see, I can't serve you as you have me." I watch their shadow on the ceiling as they dance.

10 *February*

"I'm cold," she said, and of that there was neither doubt nor a fast solution. She already wore my coat over hers, and I shivered, too wet to even bother with my own thermal issues.

I might have just turned around, but she was determined to run, and I could not imagine leaving her alone. Her house had become unsafe, and in a place like this, that made everything unsafe. And I understood. I understood perfectly. I just wished that it was not February.

A long hour later a church rose out of the fields. One of those tiny places that the priest might come to every other Sunday. We both knew that it would be locked tight. We both knew that did not matter to me. Perhaps my first level of appeal was as someone supremely useful to people who needed to evade rules.

Inside we climbed to the small balcony above the doors after I had searched out every votive that I could find and a pile of vestments and altar cloths. Within a circle of flickering light we buried ourselves beneath these sacred fabrics, and slowly let our bodies warm each other.

A History of Irish Dreams

In that moment when I have woken up – still in those most dark hours - but can not yet be truly sure of consciousness, sounds come to me, drifting on a breeze of memory, floating past my eyes, and just touching my ear-drums like the gentlest whisper of an exhausted lover. They might be a very light slop of the wind and moon pushing the river against the quays, the rhythms muffled and shaken by their paths along the stone streets and alleys to a bedroom window from decades long lost. They might be the deepest bass notes of APC tyres thundering along paving stones, with the gentlest overlay of the high-pitched notes of barbed wire vibrating on an e-chord. They might be the deep breaths of a woman long ago or yet more recent, a siren's high-low echoing from far away but coming closer, the fall of a never forgotten early May rainstorm, a sound we all know must have been a gunshot, or of the door closing as my father came home, or of my mother's feet pacing from kitchen to front window in fear.

And then I am awake, and the ceiling is above me, and the light of the always-on television provides the room with a slightly dangerous glow. I will get out of bed. I will stare out the window at the emptiness of the street below. I will go downstairs. I will consider pouring a beer down my throat. I will even open the refrigerator, and hold the bottle in my hand. I will consider just getting up. Making coffee. Sitting down and being productive again in these early hours, and writing. Sometimes I will even do one or the other of those. But usually not. Usually I will not make coffee. Usually I will put the beer back. Usually I will go back upstairs and climb back under the quilt and let my head fall into the pillow. Usually I will fall back asleep. Sometimes this will all happen two or three times in a night.

The field up at St. Peter's was not much of a field when I was a kid. What's that old *Father Ted* joke? "It's not really a field, just a place with fewer stones"? Really it is not much of a field now. But it is what we had, and so we played there. Hours upon hours, all ages mixed together mostly, some-times twenty or more boys on a team. It did not matter. You did not touch the ball much, unless you were both older and very, very good. And tougher too – but that was always understood. When I got older and close to very good I did get to touch the ball often, although it was, most assuredly, nothing equal to the brilliant George Best moves I had dreamt as a boy. But by then the games happened much less often. Mothers kept the younger ones hidden inside believing that was how they could be protected. And the best had disappeared behind ski masks or into internment or into exile. And then we could not really even go to The Brandywell anymore, and Geordie went to play for some team in Los Angeles and then, just fell into drink. We all do, do we not? And there was not enough hope around us to build new dreams. So it is those original fantasies that still creep along my vision's perimeter when I pass a field of boys kicking the football around.

When I think of that one weekend, and I think of it often, I call it the "Camelot" weekend, though I hope not outloud. There are dreams that need to be held, to be yours alone. Then they can be much freer, and I think maybe safer too. During that season when, despite the calendar, the stones of the city had turned from warm and protective to cold, grey, and unforgiving, we ran. It was not easy. Movement was simply not easy then. We had silently slid from our bedrooms, snaked around those unbreachable city walls, staying out of the glare of Army and RUC lights. We had run and hid, and run and hid, like the camp escapees we really were. Running across the Craigovan Bridge – was it two or three in the morning? – we had lain flat on the pavement when we saw headlights coming from either direction. We knew we had to be across and through the Protestant neighborhoods and out of the city before light came, and light came quickly in these northern latitudes in early summer. It took a whole other day and night to get to the sea, to the beach, and we fell asleep curled into each other behind the dune at the strand at Portstewart. For three days while parents cried and the Provos searched because back then you could not ever have called the police, and if you had they could not have crossed into the NoGo zone anyway, we lay on the sand and splashed in the cold salt water and ran into the town to find bread and cheese, and we made love like teens do, badly and quickly – but often – and with great excitement, and we smelled of the sea and sweat and each other. Until local kids found us, and I beat one of them up, and the RUC grabbed us and drove us back to the barricades, calling her a "little pope-girl slut" and threatening to cut my bollocks off. And all parts still come to me on certain nights, though not together, the beach might be a different beach, and the bridge a different bridge, but the smells never change.

Coming to the kitchen door, yes, coming in from the back on an autumn day when the wind rose out of the north, coming straight down from the Faroes and Iceland and the pole and even if the sun had been visible it would have stopped being able to really warm me weeks ago, the thick wool sweater, the knits of my ancestors, covered with the water drops that filled the air, and my ears and face red and stinging and I would fall into the corner by the stove, the peat fire filling this room with its phrases and legends and Ma in the kitchen, the bangers sizzling in the pan, the thick sense of the mash reaching through my nostrils and into my brain and, yes, I would fall asleep there until the call to come to the table. The warmest type of moment I can summon from my past.

The places that come unsummoned are the places where the bodies lie. They never change, though the backgrounds do, and the weather, and even the faces, and who I am and what role I play in each particular film clip running during that specific REM episode. There are too many bodies. And whether they died for this reason or that, for the cause or not, they have all died of the same thing. This island is cluttered with the lost ghosts we sing to as if they are heroes. They get their revenge on us by staying close.

On those nights when I am desperate for respite I pour enough pints into my brain and when my head hits the pillow I call to the thick rains that would fall and wash everything from the ancient ways of the city. That would chase those fighting inside or at least out of sight, and I in my hiding place under the rafters, could let the world be drowned out by the drumming of God's water on my family's roof. If I am lucky, it will do it still. I will sleep til dawn and arise in pain, but in the present, and thankful for that.

the border

We are walking the ridge the long way, crossing the field of tall grasses. It rained this morning, pouring down from a deep grey sky, but now the sun has pierced the cloudbank, here, and here, and here, and the light is spinning off the raindrops which still cling to the tiny seedpods.

"My shoes are soaking," she said. "Yeah," I agreed. "Where are we going?" "Not quite certain." And I was not. At the road there'd still be a bit of evidence. A change in pavement perhaps, the base of an old sign, even the overgrown foundation of a structure, or maybe just a speed sign pointing one way with "60" on it and another one pointing the other way with "100" on that. You'd be able to make a guess. But here, it was just a difficult thing to say. Here I was trying to find a line on a map. "Thanks," she said sarcastically. "You'd be very welcome," said I.

But the fact was – we were going for her. She'd asked about a story she'd heard. One of those, "How did we ever get through that" tales. But I didn't think that I could explain without showing her. Sometimes the concepts are beyond comprehension unless you can see, and feel, and breathe in the place.

We were fourteen, perhaps, and we were scared. We were not yet revolutionaries, just wee ones exploring the world, running away, getting to places we might call our own. But not quite wee enough. Some lads grow tall early. And we did not yet understand how we could look to people trained to think of us as dangerous. No one had really told us that yet.

And we had come to a tiny cart track through a field, here at the top of the hill. And we had rested in the cool shade beside a tiny stone bridge, and let our feet cool in the slow running stream, and we'd shared fags Brian had nicked from the shop on Bishops Street and cheese Thomas had begged from his Ma.

Then Brian stood up. He was the tallest of us. He had stretched dramatically since the winter, and I suppose, his red hair flaming in that summer sun, he looked at least adolescent, if not adult, from afar.

It was from afar that a rifle shot rang across the ridge. Then another. We froze. Even Brian standing there became rock. Then a third, and we began to understand and we dove, all five of us, beneath the bridge, our hearts pounding, our breathing so loud we were sure that would be the end of us.

The holes in the overcast continue to tear, and the field where we walk is now fully alight, and there it is. The bridge even tinier than I might have remembered, the stream still dribbling beneath it. It is so insignificant, as I see it now, there is no surprise that I could not see it from afar. It is so insignificant, as I come to stand beside it, that it can hardly be imagined how this was once a line separating two warring worlds.

"We hid under here," I say, pulling her down with me, into the wet, into the cool, "All five of us. We figured they were shooting from the road way over there, but we couldn'a be sure. Then Thomas said they'd surely come looking. They'd grab a few of the Paras, he told us, cause they were scared of us, thought we were all terrorists, and so no one would come alone. But that would take some time Thomas said. He was the smart one. He was always the leader, and now he said we had to move."

"He's the one who died five years ago?" "Yeah," I say, "Cancer. I sure miss him."

She looks under the bridge, and her eyes follow the stream, the long way that we crawled, one after the other, knees and elbows in the water, as we fled, hoping we were going the right way, hoping we were staying away from roads, hoping this water drifted east and down to the Foyle on our side of the border. She is trying to see, to understand, to know why Brian remembers every detail of that moment, and I do as well.

"Did they follow you?" I shrug. I am not sure. Maybe. Maybe not. We didn'a look. They often shot without follow up. That, we learned later.

But I know it still makes no sense. It is a soft stream in a soft field on a soft day. It is idyllic. More so than even the Midwestern American fields of her youth. And the idea of Paratroopers with black-painted faces shooting with high-powered rifles at young boys is impossible for her. Which is as the world should be.

"I really cannot imagine," she says. "You must have been so terrified, I don't know if I could have moved." "I know," I tell her, wrapping my arms around her. "I'm so fucking glad that you cannot comprehend it." She smiles. "Let's go get a coffee," I say, "I think there's a pub somewhere up there." And then I add, "Just over the line."

Atlantic dream

"My ocean," I tell her, "from both sides." She stands in the wind. It rushes through her soft blond hair as her blue eyes chase things deep inside me. The Atlantic sweeps before us, the waves coming in consistent chaos. "Is it different here than there?" She is asking many questions at once. "Oh, yes," I tell her. "In New York it is gentler, warmer, even in winter, even when angry. But on this side it is deeper. It is both bluer and greyer. It is harder but it calls more strongly." She is still looking at me. I look down to dodge her gaze. Eye-to-eye can be so very difficult. "Do you ever drop the poetry shit and just talk?" "That's a pretty American question." "Or a pretty female question." "You're probably right." "You know I'm right," she announces as I sit down on a huge stone. "You should put your hood up, it's cold out here." "I'm not really cold," she says, "Is it usually this warm even now?" "I remember it as warm, but that's probably just false dreams." She laughs. "You are fucking amazing." "Thanks," I tell her, leaning to kiss her, touching the skin at the back of her neck. She whispers, "That wasn't a compliment."

A History of the Bogside

Too many pints and too much time in this dark corner and the rain washing down the windows by the front and echoed even more darkly in the mirrors behind me and I have not truly slept more than three hours of the seventy-two since I made it back home.

"The area that is now known as the Bogside was originally underwater, as the Foyle flowed around the hill of Doire, of the oak grove," said the tattered old book hidden in the bottom corner of the classroom shelf. That stream on the western side of the island, it said, came to be called, "Mary Blue's Burn. It flowed along the line of Rossville Street to the west of the Lecky Road and out into the Foyle near the bottom of Bishop Street. The burn was crossed by three causeways – probably built by monks – and these followed the lines of William Street, the Bog Road, and Stanley's Walk."

As I sit at the foot of William Street today it is not hard to see those ancient Christians, disciples of St. Patrick himself, moving along the muddy highground in their rough cloth hooded gúna. The natives came here for fresh water and fish and the wild plants that flavored their food and drink and to meet the spirits of their world. Later they came to fight the invaders and later still to live at the feet of the "British" for centuries as they squeezed out a living making first whisky and cloth, then shirts and ships and phonographs. Now my friends make hard drives, unless they have escaped elsewhere.

I have come back on one of those annual pilgrimages of redemption. Though it all looks different in fact – the houses are new, the Rossville Flats are gone, there is colour here and no barbed wire – when I walk the streets I still see the old outlines rising up from the footwalks and hear the footsteps of my friends, and the thunder of the fighters, and the shouts of frightened parents.

I have seen many people over the past three days, though I have not seen her. She is now across the river, past "The Waterside," in some pleasant new estate I am sure, with her husband and her four children, or however many still live at home. She sent me an email saying, "This time, will you see me?" And all I could answer was, "I will try."

"Throughout the nineteenth century the Bogside retained a rural feel with the type of housing and lifestyle of the inhabitants," that book had told me long ago, when I would sneak it from its spot and read that rather than focusing on maths. "Many houses were inhabited by unskilled labourers from the mountain districts of Donegal who subsidised their income by maintaining small potato patches and keeping pigs and feeding them with waste from the Abbey Street distillery. Even the Catholic skilled tradesmen who earned quite superior wages could live nowhere other than the Bogside, and often they too rented out potato patches to supplement their income."

Last night I ate bangers and mash with Cillian and his family. It was served with the kind of thick potato soup that would warm me up on nights such as this, and the smells of the kitchen were overpoweringly familiar. Cillian caught me up with where everyone has gone, as he does year after year while his wife tried to convince me to return and offered match-making support.

"You need a woman from here," she told me. "One who knows where ya come from." "American women know where I come from," I said. "Nah," she was absolute. "They think you are Irish and some happy leprechaun or some such thing. They do not know a thing about Derry."

The book had not gone much past partition. "In 1921 Derry nationalists found themselves opposing Derry's inclusion in Northern Ireland. With the northern parliament assembling in June, Derry's nationalists turned south for support but the signing of the Anglo Irish Treaty in December was greeted with dismay in the city." That stopping point was good enough. The rest of the story was personal.

I look into the mirror. The grip of the silver on the back of the glass has weakened. It makes everything look much further away. I turn back, I do not like looking in mirrors. Derry has always been the victim, I think. It is always haunted by what might have been. It is a place of dreams, but dreams unfulfilled.

Cillian and Sean and Brendan push through the door, shaking water off their heads. "He's blasted already mates," Sean announces, pointing in my direction. "Called Kate yet?" Cillian asks. "Not yet," I mumble. "Fuckin' coward," Brendan says. "Always have been," I say, realizing the reason for my exile, "always have been."

An Encyclopedia of Saints

The gay couple who lived downstairs were television producers but spent their free time, when not restoring the incredible 1846 brownstone or throwing outrageous parties, directing plays at an amateur theatre in Brooklyn Heights.

I was very young and still had the body of a swimmer then. And I had already played one of the team in *The Changing Room* in Michigan, a reference you will either understand or not, and having told my landlords this, as we ate exotic olives and prosciutto in their back garden, they made me the star of first *Equus*, and then *The Elephant Man*. *Equus* was complex and difficult and I needed to be completely naked on stage with a woman touching me without showing physical response, but *The Elephant Man* may have been the most physically high-stress thing I've ever done repeatedly. In that play, un-like the film of the same name, there is no make-up and no costuming – you just twist your almost naked body until it represents the deformity, and then you hold that for the whole first act. In the second act you get to wear a tuxedo, but you are still twisted. It is thus more about humanity than horror. More about universality than uniqueness. The play is written from the doctor's memoirs. The film from notes which John Merrick – the elephant man – made himself. I think that says a great deal about self perception.

I have many names. This is the nature of who I am. A few months ago I was sitting in the dining hall at Trinity College, which serves shite cafeteria food but does it in a place that Americans would only associate with being in a Harry Potter scene, and the guy I was talking to was from Manchester and had a similarly non-Irish set of obvious names, but he said, "How many middle names might you have?" And I said, "Four," and he said, "The same." "David Padraic Columba Finnbar," I told him. "Enda Padraic Fergus Gobain," he replied. We are so unsure of who will help that we invoke all whom we imagine might prove supportive.

Saints are important, and so are performances. Saints are our role models and performance is how we get through the day with as few scars as possible. When I was young, way back when, I could not read and was labelled, in the fashion of the time, as suffering from "minimal brain damage." My brother and sisters told me this meant that I had been dropped on my head, but not from more than three meters. But it is essential, as a kid, to seem anything but retarded, so I always pretended to be lazy and surly and crazy. This left me in much trouble, but kept my reputation as intact as it could be. Yes, everybody pretty much knew, but it wasn't what *mattered* in the neighborhood. I still wrote though. I tried letters mixed with pictures, my own hieroglyphics. Sometimes a friend wrote down what I wanted to say, but usually not. So I remembered things, and film was my literature. Now I like to claim that I am simply preserving an ancient oral tradition. There is validity in that argument.

Though I know many who have, I have never had a problem with a Priest. Not "that kind" of problem. In my experience the Catholic clergy might hit and might scold and might try to make you feel guilty about just about everything, but they also listened, and taught, and sheltered. As a child and adolescent I slept in churches more nights than I could possible count, protected and hidden from the dangers of the world. Whenever I could I slept near the statue or picture of a saint, and would try and fall into dreams by retelling myself the story. I will be eternally grateful to the Holy Catholic Church, despite all of our differences.

But there are better places than churches, sometimes, in which to find myself linked to the creator. Of course this is true in the presence of love, especially in the presence of my child, but it is also true when you stare into a night sky and look deep into the past, all the way back, perhaps, to the beginning of the universe. In the late 1970s and early 1980s in New York City I had the connections that could get me to the roof of One World Trade Center. I'd sneak up the stairway from the kitchen at Windows-on-the-World. It would be late. Long past when the Observation Deck on Two had closed. The city would twinkle and flash far below, and spread out to the far horizons. St. Brendan carried back the seeing rune stone from his travels to lands far west of Ireland, places beyond imagination, perhaps, or maybe he made it to New York, half a millennia before Leifr Eiríksson found Vinland. And St. Columba carried those visions to the already nine thousand year old community on the hill of the Oak Grove where the Foyle rushed by, carving the rock of the earth, and connecting the Celts to their gods. And both, and all, held what they knew because St. Enda had given up his anger in exchange for a gentler but more powerful tale.

Above me the aircraft warning lamps would flash from the broadcasting tower. And the universe beyond that last human work would pull me into an embrace. The light that stars sent out millions, or billions, of years before would rush toward my eyes. And I would be sure that I was not alone.

Peat

In exile in the North American Midwest I am robbed of the essential smells that gave me shelter as a child. Surely there are memories made up of images and memories made up of songs and memories made up of stories remembered as I lie in bed on the cusp of sleep. There are memories that flood the brain from tastes and those that rise out of textures that have soothed or scratched. So the right kind of mashed potatoes can make me feel truly warmed on a cold night, and black pudding is all about my father, and there is a certain spin of wool which matches the Hudson's Bay Blankets that kept the night air off our child bodies, that instantly makes me tired. But I can not find the smells.

Lake Michigan is beautiful and wondrous, but it does not smell like big water to me. There is no salt in that breeze to fill the nostrils. There is no gently rotting mix of seaweed and fish either. The scent of the truly far away does not hang there, in any version, not the slightly sour scent of the Foyle, or the cold briskness of the Donegal beaches, or the sharp notes of the salt-water marshes that define the archipelago that is New York City.

And the smell of wood burning in iron stoves is great on a cold afternoon. That is redolent of the pioneers carving their paths through the vast continental forests and of the kind of nineteenth century Americana so often depicted on Christmas cards. But it is not my odour. More than anything I miss the clinging aroma of peat burning on the grate. What could define an impoverished history more than the need to burn what is really just the earth itself? Peat doesn't truly burn anyway. It smolders and smokes and the scent covers you and wraps you. And when I smell it now, on that first night back each trip, in the pub or as I walk down a residential street, a brief reverie built on a thin trail of smoke, it ignites precious corners of my brain. The house on St. Patrick Street springs into ethereal life, with ma, the aunts, the uncles, my cousins and me running in and out, the sisters laughing, my brother learning to be the adult he would barely get to be. I can touch the hard stone of the streets climbing the hills, and the old wallpaper and the cold wood floor, and the deeply worn polish of the handrail on the stair, and the rough strength of my father's hand.

Notes:

Maps which follow the *Table of Contents* are from: CAIN – the *Conflict Archive on the Internet* at the University of Ulster (Derry City) http://cain.ulst.ac.uk/images/maps/maps.htm and the National Tourism Development Authority http://www.discoverireland.ie/ (Ireland).

Wikipedia Links: http://en.wikipedia.org/wiki/Derry - http://en.wikipedia.org/wiki/Ulster - http://en.wikipedia.org/wiki/Northern_Ireland - http://en.wikipedia.org/wiki/Republic_of_Ireland - http://en.wikipedia.org/wiki/Ireland - http://en.wikipedia.org/wiki/Troubles All content copyrighted by *Wikipedia* contributors and licensed to the public under the GNU Free Documentation License.

In *The Oak Grove* a character quotes two Seamus Heaney poems, *The Road to Derry*, and *Casualty*. *Casualty* from *Field Work* by Seamus Heaney. copyright Faber and Faber, 1979. *The Road to Derry* originally published in the *Derry Journal* (copyright by Seamus Heaney).

In *Saviour* the 1932 edition of the *Lyra Celtica* as edited by E.A. Sharp and J. Matthay, is quoted: http://www.sundown.pair.com/Sharp/Lyra%20Celtica/celtica_title.htm copyright 1998, 1999, 2000 copyright by Mary Ann Dobratz All Rights Reserved with the exception of Vol. II, The Collected Works of Fiona Macleod and Vol. V, The Selected Writings of Wm. Sharp (now in print).

In *Basic Grammar*, The Beatles' *Martha My Dear* (John Lennon/Paul McCartney) is sung. Copyright 1968 by Northern Songs, Ltd. So is their song *Savoy Truffle* (George Harrison). Copyright 1968 by Northern Songs, Ltd.

In *Watching Football* a character sings part of the Beatle's song *Love Me Do* (John Lennon/Paul McCartney). Copyright 1962 by Northern Music, Ltd.

In *The Weight* the music playing in the background is the song *The Weight* by J. R. Robertson. Copyright 1968, 1970 by Dwarf Music, Inc. As performed by The Band on their 1968 album *The Big Pink*.

In *30 January 1972* Eamonn McCann is quoted from his introduction to *No Go - A Photographic Record of Free Derry* by Barney McMonagle. Published by the Guildhall Press, Derry, Ireland BT48 0LZ http://www.ghpress.com/ and copyright by the author, 1997.

In *A Long Wednesday Night at Grianán an Aileach* the *Incipit Thochmarc Edaine* is quoted, ftp://ftp.ucc.ie/pub/celt/texts/G300012.sgml via the Corpus of Electronic Texts: a Department of History project at University College, Cork, College Road, Cork, Ireland

In *I got lost on the way from here to Bushmills* a character quotes Nick Hornby's novel *A Long Way Down*, copyright 2005 Riverhead Books.

In *Storm* there are quotes from Peter Høeg's novel *Borderliners*, copyright in English translation by Barbara Haveland by Farrar Straus & Giroux 1994,